Karma's

Season

LAREDEAUX

KARMA'S SEASON

Karma's Season

This is a work of fiction. Names, characters, businesses, places, events and incidents are either the products of the author's imagination or used in a fictitious manner. Any resemblance to actual persons, living or dead, or actual events is purely coincidental.

Published by Midnight Publications

Written by: LaRedeaux
Editing: Honorable Menchan Media
ISBN-13: 978-0-9891195-5-9
ISBN-10: 0989119556
Book Website
www.midnightpublications.com
Email: **info@laredeaux.com**
10 9 8 7 6 5 4 3 2 1
PRINTED IN U.S.A

INTRODUCTION

THE SAYING goes, "Everything happens for a reason. Every action has a reaction. Always remember that what's meant to be will always find a way to come about." O'lyn Williams believed he knew the reasons his life hadn't gone according to plan. One fate filled day led to a life filled with trials... If he could do one thing, he would go back in time to change the events that turned his life upside down.

"Yo, O'lyn, hold up, holdup. We heard Ms. Piggy has a crush on you."

"Man, please, she's just tutoring me so Coach Thomas don't make me sit out the next two games. You know Mrs. Daniels can't stand me. If I don't pass this test I won't graduate or get to play in the last couple games."

"No worries dude, we got something for you. This is going to be the prank of the year. Since Ms. Piggy has a crush on you anyway. How about you ask her to prom? There's a nice size bag inside to fit that incredibly huge snout she has."

"Yo, I don't know about this. She's not a bad person. This is too much."

"Peanut, I guess you were right, O'lyn does have a crush on her. They could be Kermit and Ms. Piggy in real life." Jermaine teased.

"Forget you, Maine. Ain't nobody crushing on Veronica. Damn. Just give me the box. Let's get this over with once and for all."

O'lyn woke in a cold sweat again. The recurring dream was happening more regularly now. He constantly dreamed that his last chance to enter the AFL failed. O'lyn knew in his heart, that day changed his entire life. He now believed Karma was definitely a bitch with a long memory.

CHAPTER ONE

What therefore God hath joined together, let not man put asunder....

I F VERONICA could change anything in the world, anything at all, it would be her decision to come home early from her brunch date with the ladies of her social club. She left her husband sleeping that early Saturday morning excited about fellowshipping with the local shelter. Clark expected her to be gone all day.

In the twelve months since marrying her husband, Veronica quickly became an expert at several things. One of those things was spending Clark's money. Her husband was an extremely wealthy businessman and Veronica didn't quite understand his line of work. He vaguely explained it as an import business, bringing merchandise into the country for resale. Clark didn't discuss his business dealings and Veronica didn't mind that at all. He provided security for her and their family to be and that was all Veronica ever wanted.

After serving at the shelter, Veronica made a couple stops to pick up last minute items for Clark and their parents. Returning home and finding driveway empty, Veronica decided not to place the presents under the tree. She would store them secretly until Christmas Eve. Their home was enormous for just the two of them. There were a total of eight bedrooms and five baths. She decided to hide her gifts in the one place she was sure Clark would never look; the attic.

Though reasonable at the time, it was a decision she would live to regret.

The attic was large, clean and uninhabited. The only thing stored there was her grandmother's old furniture. She remembered there was a large closet on the far end. It was a closet perfect for storing the gifts she'd gotten.

Veronica flew out of the Mercedes Clark gave her for a wedding present, loading her arms with bags. Angelica, their housekeeper, poked her head out the door and started to come out to help, but Veronica waved her away, dragging her packages in on her own. Taking two steps at a time, she raced to the top floor of their home and to the attic before Clark came home from wherever he'd gone to. She tugged down the ladder to the space and, with some very complicated maneuvering, managed to get all the items up without having to make a second trip. She quickly ascended the ladder, pulling it up behind her to cover her tracks.

Crossing the room, Veronica noticed; the open bay window permitted more than enough light so she wouldn't have to turn on the switch. Pulling open the closet doors, she was relieved to find it mostly empty.

Stacking the last box atop the tower she assembled in the closet, Veronica heard the sliding ladder get yanked down. Letting out a quick gasp, she prayed she hadn't been found out.

Thinking fast, she crammed herself in next to the tower of presents and slid the closet door shut behind her. It was a flimsy door that didn't lock; the kind with wooden slats and cracks between them. She could see out into the room, yet no one could see in. Veronica stifled a giggle as Clark's head ascended into the attic. She assumed he never came to the attic, so she surmised he must be there to hide her presents as well. Veronica quickly realized she was wrong when another head emerged up the stairs...then another one after that.

The first was De 'Carlo. Veronica had met him before. He was Clark's chief of security at the bar he co-owned with his brother Ryan. De 'Carlo was a large man, over 6'5" and muscular. He looked at least ten years younger than he actually was. He rarely spoke in her presence and he almost never smiled. De 'Carlo always made her nervous.

The second person, she definitely didn't recognize. She watched through the slats as De 'Carlo shoved him into a chair. Veronica slapped a hand over her mouth to stifle her gasp.

"I wish we didn't have to do this here." Her husband's voice was low and serious.

De 'Carlo gave the man in the chair a shove.

"We wouldn't if this idiot had kept his mouth shut." He ripped the bag off his head. "Most of the warehouses are hot now, thanks to him."

Clark let out a humorous laugh. "That is disappointingly true." Crossing his arms he leaned against the wall; his handsome face a mask. "It would be unfortunate if my wife were to find out."

De 'Carlo snorted as he began laying down the plastic before tying the man to the chair using the zip ties he carried in his jacket. "She still doesn't know?" Clark smiled, studying his nails. "She's not the smartest woman in the world." He watched as De 'Carlo leaned down to pick up a small case he brought with him. "But that's not the reason I married her."

Veronica's eyes narrowed at the insult. Sure, she wasn't Einstein, but Clark sounded like he thought she was an idiot. Her time in the closet was proving to be quite enlightening. Her husband was a criminal and he apparently thought she was a moron.

"So why did you?" De 'Carlo studied the man in the chair, making sure his hands and feet were securely tied. He pulled the bag off the man's head. Veronica didn't recognize him... He was a terrified, raggedy looking man with a gag in his mouth.

Clark arched an eyebrow. "Her father was an unfortunate card player and have you seen her?" He turned towards the table and opened the small case they'd brought with them. "Our children will be beautiful; that's a guarantee. Let's hope they get my intelligence, though. One beautiful idiot is quite enough."

Veronica scowled. She could feel her temperature elevate with every word spoken. Her divorce was imminent. In fact, she was a step away from jumping out of the closet and demanding one when she saw what Clark had in his hand.

Her electric carving knife.

The man in the chair began to scream under his gag, his muffled wails carrying throughout the room. Clark handed the carving knife to De 'Carlo and leaned down over the man. He snatched the gag out of his mouth, loosening a few teeth in the process.

"Now, Herman," Clark's voice was ice cold. It was the same voice he used when Angelica used the wrong starch on his shirts. "Perhaps you can explain to me why all my warehouses are currently under surveillance?"

Poor Herman gasped; his swollen lips held dried blood, his eyes were red and teary. He never took them off the carving knife. "I swear, Mr. Torres, I told no one. I swear on my children's lives."

"If you mean your twins, Olivia and Sophia, there is no need." Clark pulled the carving knife from De 'Carlo's hand. "It seems your children had an ill-fated mishap this morning in your pool, along with their mother. So you see," Clark studied the knife disinterestedly, "you swearing on their lives means very little to me, considering they are no longer alive."

Herman began to wail as the meaning of Clark's words sunk in. Veronica shoved a hand in her mouth to stifle her own shocked sob. Her husband wasn't just a criminal; he was a ruthless murderer who apparently had no problem eliminating children or women. How could she not have known?

"Now," Clark leaned closer as the wailing man gasped, trying to regain his breath. "Now that your quality of life has taken another downward spiral you'll have two choices." He ran the carving knife down Herman's face. "You will never leave this house alive, anyway. However, the choice is yours. You can tell me exactly who you spoke to and receive a quick death, followed by being dismembered and dumped into a shallow grave. Or, we can dismember you while you're still alive, or at least until you feel like talking."

Veronica watched Herman. His eyes were empty and dejected now that he knew his family was gone, and he would soon be joining them. His expression was stoic. He glared into her husband's eyes and then, to Veronica's surprise, he spat a bloody mixture into Clark's face.

Veronica flinched, but Clark just looked annoyed. He pulled a handkerchief from his pocket and wiped the spittle away, his eyes never leaving Herman. He handed the carving knife to De 'Carlo. "Start with his fingers."

Veronica clamped her hands over her ears as the carving knife whirred to life. Even pressing them down as hard as she could, she still heard the scream of the knife as it cut into the meat of Herman's hand, severing through bone and muscle. He was screaming, but the sound of the knife drowned everything out.

For the next two hours, Veronica sat in a closet surrounded by gifts, watching as her husband and De 'Carlo dismembered a man alive.

O'lyn Williams pulled into a Circle K store just outside of Jacksonville, Florida, as the air pressure in his right front tire dropped yet again. Sighing he pushed open the driver's side door, preparing to pull out the hand crank inflator he'd bought discounted at a local Wal-Mart. It would take forever and was hell on his shoulder, but he had no choice. All the cheaper repair shops closed hours ago. He couldn't afford road-side service. If he continued, he was guaranteed to have a blow-out.

That's just the way karma works, like a wayward bitch, striking like a thief in the night when you least expected it.

After high school, O'lyn had been plagued with a continuing string of bad luck. If something bad could happen, it happened to O'lyn Williams. His promising football career ended by a senseless freak accident. Then, he'd gone to community college, only to drop out after a minor marijuana conviction nullified his financial aid. Unsure of what to do, O'lyn turned to the military, certain that an athletic fella like him could have a great career soldier.

As luck would have it, he suffered from night blindness – the one medical malady that couldn't be waived to get him into service anyway. Even the most basic soldier had to be able to see proficiently at night. O'lyn couldn't even do that.

O'lyn wasn't a particularly smart man, nor was he particularly charismatic. The few things he had going for him included being naturally handsome and naturally athletic.

While those qualities alone were enough to make him the king of high school, he'd learned they'd grown exceedingly useless the closer he got to thirty.

O'lyn flinched as he stubbed his toe on a rock on the way to his trunk, but kept moving. He ran his hand over his wavy low cut hair and pulled open the hatchback, yanking out the hand pump grudgingly. He walked back around to the front of the jeep, stubbing his toe again on the same damn rock. He bent down, overcome by stifling humidity, and let out a muffled swear as he realized he was sweating buckets in his last clean shirt. He started pumping and pumping, grunting with exertion as he struggled to get his slowly leaking tire above 30 psi.

"This your car?"

O'lyn sighed inwardly and turned around to be confronted with the navy blue, starched leg of a Florida

State Trooper. He wanted to say, *No, I'm just siphoning air out of someone else's tire.* Instead, he stretched to his full 6'3 height and met the state troopers glare head on. "Yeah, it's mine."

The trooper scowled at O'lyn and pulled out his ticket book. "Your registration is expired." He snarled.

O'lyn nodded in agreement. "I'm planning on getting it registered when I settle."

The state trooper pulled out his pen with a click he started to write the ticket. "And where you planning on settling?"

O'lyn was about to say 'Memphis' when he noticed the trooper had those penetrating grey-green eyes. "*Her eyes*" eyes that always had an effect on him, regardless of the owner. They always hit him with the same amount of guilt he'd felt that day in high school, nearly thirteen years before. He always thought of Veronica Brown.

That sad image of those grey-green eyes, strangely beautiful in her homely face, haunted him years later.

O'lyn hoped she would go to her reunion. He had just gotten the news that he didn't make the AFL team, The New Orleans Voodoo. The only reason he'd gone at all was to see her again. To tell her he was sorry and that, weirdly, he'd missed her; the homely, overweight girl with the awkward crush. The girl he destroyed for no more reason when he found her crush embarrassing and he was angry with her.

She hadn't gone to the reunion. Her name tag, with her maiden name in parenthesis, sat unclaimed on the table all night. He was surprised to learn she'd gotten married. He doubted she had aged well. She was probably even heavier at 28 than she had been at 16. He pictured her husband as an overweight, balding man with a large hook nose.

Her new last name was Spanish. It made sense, considering she fled their hometown shortly after graduation and settled down in Coastal Georgia. He wondered if she was happy, if she had children. He wondered if she still dwelled on high school the way he did. It wouldn't surprise him if she did. She had, after all, been the victim.

"You on something, son?"

O'lyn looked up, shaken out of his thoughts. "No, sir. Just overheated. Sure is hot here." O'lyn tugged at the collar of his t-shirt uncomfortably, staring up at the afternoon sun. His thoughts stayed with Veronica. The more he thought about it, the more his mind stuck to that day. It was shortly after the day he'd humiliated her in front of the entire school that his luck had started to go bad. "I'm going to Memphis, sir."

"Right," The trooper nodded and pointed to the curb. "Can you come over here for me?" O'lyn nearly growled in frustration as the trooper started to guide him through a field sobriety test. As he said his alphabet backwards, he thought more and more about Veronica. Her sad, grey eyes and her broken heart. The way everything had gone perfectly for him before that day, and how it had all turned to shit afterwards. Perhaps it had been karma?

"Follow my pen, son."

O'lyn followed the pen, but his mind stayed elsewhere. He was down to his last $500, no job prospects in sight, driving a broken-down jeep and living on a wardrobe of five different shirts and two pairs of jeans. Maybe his jeep broke down for a reason. Maybe karma was telling him that if he wanted to move forward, if he wanted anything good to happen again, he needed to go back. He needed to apologize to Veronica Brown, the girl he'd once liked so much and hurt so badly. What could it hurt? He had nowhere else to be. As he hopped on one foot down a straight line, he turned his face to the trooper. "How far is Savannah, Georgia from here?"

The trooper looked at him in confusion. "Georgia?" He tilted his head in thought. "About an hour and a half."

O'lyn dropped his foot to the ground. He was less than two hours from Veronica. What would it hurt to alter his course and see if an apology would actually work?

"Why do you ask?"

O'lyn snapped his attention back to the trooper. "There's a girl I know; from high school..."

Suddenly, the stern trooper's face slid into an easy smile. "First love, huh?"

"Something, like that."

"Well, that explains why you've been so distracted." The trooper smiled and closed his ticket book, seeming to forget he was about to issue a ticket for an expired registration. "I married my high school sweetheart. Best choice I ever made was hunting her down and knocking on her door."

O'lyn watched in amazement as the trooper walked around his jeep, forgetting about the sobriety test and instead, getting stuck in his own love story. "She's in Savannah. I figured it never hurts to try again."

The trooper nodded, "Yeah, but you're not going to get there on this tire." The trooper kicked the leaky front driver's side tire on O'lyn's truck. "But my brother-in-law just bought a new car and has been selling the parts off his old jeep. Pretty sure one of his tires would fit yours."

O'lyn's eyebrow shot up. *Could karma work this fast?* "Do you think he'd be willing to sell them cheap, because I don't have a lot of money?"

The trooper shook his head. "Consider it on me."

Shocked, O'lyn got into his broken-down jeep and followed the trooper to a modest, family community in Jacksonville. The now genial state trooper introduced him to his brother-in-law and they soon had the front tire on O'lyn's jeep changed, free of charge. Pulling out of the dirt driveway and onto the road, he smiled and waved to the brother-in-law and the closet romantic state trooper. He was going to find Veronica Brown-Torres and he was going to fix what he'd done wrong.

For the first time in a little over thirteen years, he felt like he was finally on the right path.

Veronica sat across from her husband, nervously fidgeting with her fork and avoiding eye contact. Everything felt surreal, like she was walking through a dream. After her husband and De 'Carlo had finished with the body, they had left it, presumably expecting the 'idiot' Veronica to be home any minute. She'd waited for 30 terrifying minutes, alone with the mutilated body of Herman, until she finally had the courage to brave her way out of the attic.

She slipped out unnoticed and spent the afternoon driving around town, going nowhere, doing nothing. She drove in a blank, humdrum haze, unsure of what to do or if she could do anything at all.

She wouldn't and couldn't go to the cops. She had witnessed first-hand what happened to people who talked about her husband.

"The chicken is a little tough."

Please don't kill Angelica. "I think it's just the cut." *Oh, God...I said cut.* Veronica's heart started to race again.

Clark shoved his plate away. "Probably, tell Angelica to start shopping at a different butcher. This is the third time this week."

Veronica offered a silent prayer that Clark wouldn't kill the butcher for his subpar selection. She nodded wordlessly.

"How was shopping?"

It was going great until I came home and witnessed your barbaric mutilation of someone. "It was fine."

Clark took a sip of his wine, still watching her carefully. "Have you decided what you want for Christmas, yet?"

Yes, a divorce...and please don't kill me. "No." She shook her head, trying to get the sound of an electric carving knife cleaving through bone out of her thoughts. She started to clear her plate. "I'm not feeling very well. I think I might go lay down."

Clark gave her a gentle smile. "Too much shopping?"

Too much watching my husband and his henchmen commit murder. "Something like that." Veronica could feel her husband's eyes burning into her back as she walked up the stairs.

She wondered how long it would be until he got tired of his idiot wife and she got her turn with the carving knife.

O'lyn checked the address for the third time. According to his GPS, this was where Veronica now lived with her husband, Clark Torres. It was better than he'd expected; much better. O'lyn had expected a one-bedroom, tiny house in a rough part of town. Instead, he was looking at a two-story mini mansion with a Lexus and Mercedes in the driveway.

Veronica had done very well for herself, indeed.

He slid out of the driver's seat and walked up the cobblestone path lined by immaculate flowerbeds. Veronica's home was located in an exclusive gated community. Luckily for him, the elderly security guard had mistaken him for the pool cleaner and let him in without question. He had been afraid to give his name at the gate. He was afraid Veronica would hear it and refuse to see him.

O'lyn took a deep breath as he raised the brass door knocker and rapped on the door. He barely knocked once when the door was pulled open and a short, middle aged, heavyset woman was smiling at him.

"Veronica?" O'lyn stared at her in shock. He'd expected her to age poorly, but not at twice the rate of a normal person. Her hair was still deep auburn, but it was streaked with grey. Her eyes were hidden behind heavy bifocals. Before he could get another word out, the woman turned away.

"Mrs. Torres, you have a visitor." The woman had a Spanish accent and O'lyn felt a little stupid for mistaking her for Veronica. His nerves were getting the better of him.

"Who is it?" He heard the sound of approaching footsteps; the soft soprano voice.

Then she was there.

If it wasn't for her unique grey eyes, he would have never recognized her. She had lost the weight; that was clear. The chubby pear-shaped body and ugly, bulky clothes were gone. She was wearing a form-fitting pink halter top and a pair of tight low rise jeans. She had the body of a Jet centerfold with a tiny waist, rounded hips and full breasts. Her hair was cut short, in a chin length, streaked-layered bob that exposed high cheekbones, full lips and a perfect nose.

The nose was definitely the result of a very skilled plastic surgeon. The Veronica he'd known had a wide beak of a nose. "Veronica?"

She crossed her arms over her chest and watched him cautiously. "Yeah?"

The words were out of his mouth before he could stop them. "My God, you look amazing!"

She rolled her eyes. "Tell me something I don't know." A hand dropped on a curvy hip. "Look, if you're trying to flatter me to get me to buy something, it won't work."

O'lyn shook his head, surprised she hadn't recognized him. "No, Veronica; it's me, O'lyn." Veronica's grey eyes gave no hint of remembering who he was. "O'lyn Williams?" Still, nothing chimed in Veronica's memory. "From high school?" He was starting to feel like an idiot.

"High school?" Veronica shook her head. "I didn't go to high school here; I went in ..."

"Louisiana," he finished for her. "I know." O'lyn raked his hand through his hair in frustration. "That's why I'm here...the reason I've come to beg for your forgiveness, I have to apologize to you."

"Apologize?" Veronica tilted her head in confusion. "Are you the guy who hit our mailbox and drove away?" She put up a hand as he started to speak again. "Look, its fine. But let's just forget it happened, ok? My husband was kind of obsessed about that and if he finds out who did it, he'll probably flip out."

"No, I..." This meeting was not going as O'lyn had planned. Veronica seemed to have no memory at all. If anything, she seemed distracted and anxious. She also seemed to be in a big hurry to get him off her doorstep. "Are you okay?"

Veronica nearly laughed at the stranger's question. Okay? She would never be okay again! Her husband was a murderer and she was a terrible actress.

All night, she struggled, pretending she was fine and nothing was wrong, but Clark was starting to catch on. He'd been shooting her peculiar looks and they were making her even more nervous, which made her act even more strangely.

It was a vicious cycle that was going to get her killed. She still had no idea what to do. She couldn't go to the police. He husband wasn't just a killer, he was a Kingpin. She had seen how that movie ended and she had no desire to wind up a bag of body parts floating down the Savannah River.

She could run. The idea had come and gone a few times. She originally planned to pretend nothing had happened, but she knew she would never be able to pull it off. Even a stranger standing on her doorstep could tell there was something wrong with her. She had to run.

Veronica was vaguely aware she had been silent for an awkward amount of time, but she didn't care. She wasn't upset about the mailbox and she hoped O'lyn or whoever he was would just take her forgiveness and move on. He was the last thing she needed now.

She would run, she finally decided. She would run and she wouldn't take anything with her that belonged to Clark. She still had her savings account from her grandmother. She could get by on that until she found out what she was going to do. She'd leave his credit cards, his car, even the purse he'd gotten her for her last birthday.

If he saw she wasn't going to take anything of his and she wasn't going to cause any trouble for him, maybe he'd let her go. It was a long shot, but it was the only shot she had. Now, she just had to figure out how to get to town.

"Veronica?"

She looked up at the stranger. Then she looked behind him, to the jeep parked in the street in front of her house. Her words came out in a rush. "If I forgive you for the mailbox, will you give me a ride to the city?"

"Mailbox?" He shook his head again. "Veronica, this isn't about your mailbox."

She nearly screamed in frustration. What was with this guy? "Fine, whatever it's about. Will you give me a ride the city?"

"Look, I don't know what's going on," he finally seemed to notice the desperation in her eyes, because he relented. "Fine, I'll take you to the city. I'll take you anywhere you want to go."

Veronica let out a sigh of relief. "Thanks," She turned towards the stairs. "Just wait right there; please don't leave! I'll only be a few minutes."

He nodded and Veronica raced up the stairs, worried he would leave before she returned. He was her only hope. She had no idea when Clark would be back and cabs left a trail. She needed him. With her heart thundering in her chest, she raced into the bedroom she and Clark shared. She started stripping off the clothes she'd bought with his money. She took everything off and began rummaging through the drawers for clothes that had been hers since before they got married. After a few minutes, she was lucky enough to find an old NOLA t-shirt, a pair of poorly-fitting jeans and a sweatshirt.

She had no underwear. Clark had insisted on only high-end lingerie after they were married, and had tossed all her old cotton briefs. None of her prior undergarments made the cut.

Yanking open her purse, she found her driver's license and the picture of her mother she always carried. She stuffed them in the back pocket of her jeans. Finally, she found the bank book from her old savings account and grabbed that, too.

She had nothing on her that didn't belong to her, except for her wedding ring. With eyes that were surprisingly teary, she yanked at the wedding band set. She had a moment of panic when they refused to budge. It would all be for nothing if he thought she had stolen the ring. The gaudy diamond was easily worth six figures. She pulled again and the ring mercifully came loose.

With hands shaking so hard they hurt, she dropped the ring on their dresser and made her way back downstairs. She could only pray he was still waiting for her.

O'lyn stood in the doorway of Veronica's home, waiting for her return. She raced down the stairs, dressed differently than she had been before. The sexy clothes were gone and, instead, she was wearing a pair of jeans too big for her, a faded t-shirt and, if he wasn't mistaken from the jiggle he was seeing when she walked, she was no longer wearing a bra.

"You ready?"

She nodded happily and started to march out the door in front of him.

"You don't need a purse or anything?"

She slapped the back pocket of her ill-fitting jeans. "Got everything I need right here."

O'lyn shook his head and followed her out the door. His apology was definitely not going as planned.

CHAPTER TWO

O'LYN'S PASSENGER stared at him. He could feel her eyes on his face, studying him. Finally, she spoke.

"Hey!" Her pretty grey eyes were wide. "I went to high school with you!"

O'lyn let out a laugh at her statement. "As I was trying to tell you."

"Hmmph," She flopped back in her seat, her pretty face scrunched up in thought. "What a weird coincidence."

"Coincidence?"

"Yeah," She gestured towards him. "The guy who flattened our mailbox was someone I went to high school with. Small world."

O'lyn let out a snort of frustration. Her looks had changed, but Veronica was just as flakey as she'd been in high school. "I didn't run over your mailbox!"

"Oh," she shot him a hurt look. "Well you don't have to yell at me over it. You were the one who was apologizing for running it over."

O'lyn took a deep breath and let it out again. "I wasn't apologizing for running over your mailbox. I was apologizing for the way I treated you in high school."

"Really?" Veronica thought back to high school. Vague memories of being a chubby subject of ridicule, going home alone every day after school to listen to music, to take care of her various pets, and hold her mother's hand when the pain got too bad played in her mind like a carousel. "That was like a million years ago."

"It was thirteen years for me. Ten years for you. You just had your high school reunion." O'lyn's frustration was coming out in his voice, even though he was trying to hide it.

Veronica didn't miss it. "For someone trying to apologize, you're kind of being a jerk about the whole thing."

He gestured to the road. "I'm giving you a ride."

"True," Veronica pressed her forehead to the passenger side window and watched the scenery fly past. "Well, once you drop me off, you can consider all forgiven and all your sins absolved."

O'lyn considered her statement, wondering what his newfound karma god would think of that. Finally, he shook his head negatively. "You can't forgive me for something you don't remember."

Veronica rolled her eyes, shooting him a look. "Look, I'm deeply sorry I don't remember your taunts in high school. I had a large list of tormentors and honestly, all their faces have kind of blurred together. So you can either accept the forgiveness or you could go on feeling guilty for the rest of your life. I don't care either way." Her eyes fell onto the open road again. "I have bigger problems right now than remembering high school. If I could, I would go back to high school a million times over, if it would get me out of the situation I'm in right now."

Her voice was so sad, O'lyn turned to look at her. "Anything I can help with?"

She shook her head. "The only thing you can help with is bringing me where I need to go and dropping me off."

O'lyn shook his head and focused on the road again. "Where are we going anyway?"

"Tatemville."

Clark Torres arrived home to a strangely silent house. "Veronica?" His voice echoed off the quiet walls. It was 7 pm and Angelica was long gone, leaving him and his wife alone for the evening. "Veronica, kitten. I'm home early." He tossed his keys on the table. "Time to work on that baby you owe me."

Clark raised his eyebrow as the silence of the room mocked him. It was unusual for Veronica to not come bounding down the stairs as soon as he opened the door, ready to hop into his arms. It was especially unusual of Veronica to not respond to him when he called for her.

He started to wonder if she was sick. She'd been acting strangely the night before. He headed up the stairs to investigate; sure she was lying in their bed asleep. He pushed open the door to the master suite. "Veronica, darling, you okay?"

It was deserted. The lights were out and their king sized bed was still made. It hadn't been slept in.

"Veronica?" Clark was starting to get nervous. Veronica never stayed out late on a Sunday and she'd never left the house without leaving him a note. His eyes dropped to the floor. The clothes Veronica had been wearing when he'd left were in a pile on the floor. More unusual behavior. Veronica never left anything lying around. She was almost compulsively neat. His eyes fell on the dresser they shared. Antique, polished oak. It cost him a pretty penny to purchase. But Veronica wanted it, had given him those big, grey kitten eyes that made him melt every time.

And he'd broken out his black card.

It wasn't just the dresser he was staring at, though. It was the object sitting on top of it. A platinum gold, princess cut 4.5 carat pink diamond wedding ring. It had cost him a fortune and he picked it out himself. The second he saw it, he thought of her. She'd loved it. She never took it off.

Until today.

He marched towards the dresser and snatched the ring up, marveling at how tiny it looked in his large hand. When Veronica wore it, it looked gigantic. He liked the way it looked on her, liked the way anyone could see from a mile away she was taken. She was his.

He pulled out his cell phone and pressed 3 on his speed dial. De 'Carlo picked up before the first ring was over. "I need you here now." He glared at the ring in his hand, determined to glue it on to his beautiful wife's finger the second he found her, so she could never take it off again. *It seems my wife has decided to leave me.*

O'lyn leaned forward, reading the peeling paint on the door. "Brake Pad?"

They were parked outside the former garage turned bar in one of the rougher neighborhoods in Savannah. O'lyn was actually pretty surprised Veronica would want to come here. He expected to drop his pampered princess off at a Four Seasons, where she could run up her husband's credit card in revenge for whatever fight they were having. Instead, they were idling in front of a dilapidated bar, on a deserted street filled with empty businesses and bums loitering in the alleyway.

"Yes," Veronica reached for her door handle and shot him a nervous smile. "Thanks so much for driving me here. And like I said, whatever you did, you're totally forgiven now."

O'lyn watched Veronica pensively, wondering if what he'd done was enough to satisfy the karma gods and make his life normal again. He watched her push her way out of the jeep and stroll to the sidewalk in front of the bar, with a determined air. Shaking his head, he put his hand to the key in the ignition, planning on gunning the engine and getting the hell out of dodge. Just as he was turning the key, a blue spark of static electricity attacked his hand so bad that his thumb went numb. *"Ok, fine, we're not done yet."* O'lyn muttered as he turned off the engine and pushed open his door. He took a brief look around and could kind of understand where karma was coming from. He was inclined to agree. There was no way in hell he was leaving the sheltered Veronica in an area of town like this. Even in her cheaper clothes, everything about her screamed money, from her perfectly styled hair to her perfectly manicured hands. She could be raped and murdered in a matter of hours.

Veronica looked back as she realized O'lyn was following her. "I'm fine," Veronica shot a nervous look to the bar. "I have friends here."

He walked around to her side of the car and caught her by the elbow. "You have friends here?"

Veronica   cleared her throat. "Well, I have a friend here." Pulling out of his grip, she headed towards the door. O'lyn flinched as she pushed it open. The hinges hadn't been oiled in years and the door screamed in protest over being moved out of its slightly open/slightly closed state.

"Veronica..." O'lyn started to speak, but she was already shoving herself into the bar. He followed her in. The inside matched the outside. It was broken down; the smell of rotting wood, cigarette smoke and old grease hanging heavily in the air. In the center of the bar, two men sat at a creaky, shaking table, playing a game of blackjack. One was middle-aged, with black hair starting to grey at the temple. He was the definition of ruggedly handsome.

The other man defied description. Even seated, O'lyn could tell he was the approximate size of a refrigerator. He was midnight black, completely bald and completely expressionless. One of the man's eyes was pitch black; so dark, the pupil was no longer discernable. The other was covered in an eye patch.

If Veronica was claiming she had a friend here, O'lyn was seriously starting to worry about what he was getting himself into. Both the men turned towards them when they walked in and were eyeing them with open hostility. O'lyn was just starting to prepare for a fight, when a new voice rang out.

"Ronniiii!" They both spun as a bleached blond woman in her mid-forties rounded the bar. "It's about time you came to check out the new digs!" The woman was pretty, but in an incredibly rough way. Her hair was two shades of blonde, with a good four inches of dark roots sticking out of the top. A four-inch scar ran from right under her right nostril all the way up to her ear. Her eyes were bloodshot, as though she'd been up for a long period of time.

Veronica let out a sigh of relief next to him and the men went back to their chess game. "Mech!" O'lyn watched in shock as his princess raced around the curve of the mahogany bar to hug the blonde woman. "I've missed you so much! You really have to stop disappearing."

Mechico gave a crooked smile. "It's kind of my thing."

"But six months?"

Mech sighed. "What can I say? Mistakes were made, money was stolen." She waved a hand clutching a cigarette. "It's all water under the bridge."

Her eyes met O'lyn's and for a second, he was taken aback. Her gaze was familiar. Her eyes were eyes he'd seen before. They were the eyes of a loan shark threatening to take his legs if the debt wasn't repaid. They were the eyes of a cowboy on his last ride. They were dangerous eyes.

Whoever this Mech was, she was more than a bartender.

She took a drag off her cigarette, eyeing him with suspicion. "Who's this?"

He reached out a hand to shake. "I'm O'lyn Williams, ma'am."

She looked at his hand as though he'd extended a snake. "Ma'am?" She shot her gaze to the table across the bar, focusing on the dark-haired man with her same bloodshot eyes. "Beast, am I old enough to be a ma'am?"

"In my mind, you're always twelve, Mech."

Mechico sighed, "Such is my life." She looked Veronica deep in the eye. "Tell me, what is the point of being a criminal mastermind when you can't even get the respect of your own uncle?" She turned back towards the bar. "So, what are you running from, pretty, pretty Veronica?" Mech took another drag off her cigarette.

Veronica let out a nervous giggle. "Who said I was running?"

Mech snorted. "I know the look of hunted prey when I see it."

Veronica swallowed deeply and shot a look to O'lyn. "Can we talk in private?"

Mech yanked up the partition in the bar and gestured Veronica in. "Sure thing. We can use my workroom. Thanks to my new assistant, it is almost 100% rat free."

Veronica started to follow her and O'lyn caught her arm again. "No." No way was karma god okay with Veronica disappearing into the bowels of a criminal's hideout. He was sure that's where he was now. This was no regular bar and these were no regular people. His brief stint in county jail had taught him how to recognize the seedy underworld when he saw it. Veronica didn't belong in it.

Veronica glared at him. "Listen, I've already forgiven you. It's already in the past." She waved a hand towards the door. "You can go now with your conscience completely absolved, ok?" She looked to where the clearly insane Mech was waiting to lead her down to her 'rat free' workroom. "She can help me now." Veronica tried to tug her arm free. "You can't."

"I might be able to if you would tell me what's wrong." O'lyn was no longer convinced that Veronica was a spoiled millionaire's wife trying to get revenge on her husband. She was clearly scared and clearly in over her head, if she was considering mixing up with the likes of Mech and her Uncle Beast.

Veronica let out a sigh, her face filled with tension and frustration. "Look, I'll be fine." Her voice was soothing. It was a voice she had used before, and it had always worked to calm Clark down when he got upset about something. Weirdly, O'lyn wasn't buying it. She tried again. "It's nothing you need to involve yourself in."

O'lyn was firm. "You're not going anywhere without me."

Veronica gave a heartfelt sigh and turned back towards Mech. "Do you mind if he comes?"

Mech watched O'lyn carefully and took a drag off her cigarette. "I don't care who comes, so long as I get paid." She watched as Veronica nodded and walked down the stairs to her mysterious workroom. Mech threw up an arm and blocked O'lyn's way before he could follow her, the nonchalance gone.

"I know how to choke a man with his own shirt." She turned to O'lyn, sucking another drag off her cigarette. O'lyn tried to shove his way past her and Mech gave him a smirk. He tilted his head and realized the two men playing a game of cards were no longer playing. They were standing and watching him, waiting for his next move. "And I have Pit's in the basement." Another drag. O'lyn knew, just by looking at Mech – this was her house and he would play by her rules, even if he didn't know what they were, yet.

O'lyn clenched his fists, his entire body wanting to go into fight mode, despite the fact that he knew he was outmatched. Since learning that Veronica was in serious trouble, and not throwing a spoiled rich wife tantrum, something primal in him had woken up. Something that told him to protect her at all costs. His nostrils flared and he leaned down to meet Mech nose to nose, not caring about what she or her patrons could do to him. Not if she was going to keep him from Veronica. His voice was cold and grave when he spoke again. "I only want to help her."

To his surprise, Mech raised her arm and let him pass. Right as he began to move past her, she met his gaze dead-on and gave him a conspirator's wink. "Haven't you ever heard the road to hell is paved with good intentions?"

"I swear, she was completely faithful." A terrified man sat in the wingchair in his living room, looking up at a furious Clark. Marcus, the man being interrogated, had been hired for one thing and one thing only. To follow his Veronica and to ensure that she stayed committed to him and only him.

To date, all of Marcus' reports had been mundane. Veronica went to the store. Veronica was learning how to paint. Veronica is taking yoga, Pilates and kickboxing classes. Veronica was learning French and Spanish.

That part had touched him.

But, in every single one of Marcus' reports, 'Veronica has taken a lover', had never been a subject line. As far as the man hired to watch his wife was concerned, Veronica was as innocent as the driven snow.

Clark leaned forward, his dark eyes flashing. "Then why the hell is Angelica telling me that she took off with some man yesterday?" Clark was furious. On discovering his missing wife, he'd opened his own investigation, complete with every henchman at his disposal. He'd always had Veronica watched and she'd never disappointed him. She didn't cheat; she didn't flirt. She seemed entirely oblivious that other men existed at all.

He shot a furious look at his housekeeper. "Tell it again."

Angelica clutched her napkin she'd been using to nervously clean his dining room table, despite the fact that it was spotless. "A man came to the door. He said something about the mailbox. Veronica left with him."

Clark growled in frustration and grabbed a vase that had been sitting on the table. He studied it for a moment and then suddenly, tossed it across the room, watching in mild satisfaction as it smashed against the far wall. Everyone but De 'Carlo flinched. Then, as quickly as his temper tantrum started, it was over. He turned back to his quarry, Marcus, looking strangely calm. "So he destroyed my mailbox and stole my wife?"

Marcus leaned forward in his chair. "Mr. Torres, I swear, she never gave any indication." Marcus swallowed as Clark's furious eyes landed on him. "She only went shopping yesterday. I never lost sight of her once. She went to a few stores and then drove back home." Marcus let out a nervous laugh. "I could even tell you every single one of the Christmas presents she got for you."

Clark considered his statement. "Christmas presents?"

Marcus nodded, desperate to make his boss understand. "Yes. As far as I could tell, she was shopping for you all day yesterday."

Clark swallowed as an idea started to form. "What time did she come home?"

"Around three. The housekeeper tried to help her unpack, but Veronica wouldn't let her. She took all the bags she had and went back inside." Marcus

KARMA'S SEASON   66

took a deep breath. "After that, I left, because it looked like she was home for the night anyway."

He focused his dark gaze on Angelica. "It is true, Mr. Torres. She brought in gifts for you, but wouldn't let me help. I think she was going to hide them."

Clark cleared his throat. "Hide them where, Angelica?"

Angelica watched him nervously, still twisting the napkin in her hands. "In the attic, I think."

Clark's eyebrow shot up. It couldn't be possible. He met De 'Carlo's eyes and nodded towards the upper floor.

De 'Carlo followed close behind him as he headed for the second floor. "Do you really think she saw?"

Clark didn't answer him. Instead, he yanked down the attic ladder and ascended before De 'Carlo could cut in front of him. The room had been cleaned, the body removed, but still, the metallic scent of blood clung in the air. He looked around for a hiding place and his gaze fell on the brown slatted folding door of a closet that he and Veronica had never used. It was too inconvenient.

With De 'Carlo hot on his heels, Clark yanked open the sliding door. Inside, he found a haphazardly stacked pile of presents. The arm of a cardigan was dangling out of one of the bags; a new set of golf clubs was sticking out of the other. In the middle of the massive mountain of gifts, he saw a small indentation. It was just the size of Veronica's curvy body. He pulled the door shut and peered through the slats to confirm his suspicion.

His wife had seen everything.

CHAPTER THREE

VERONICA FOCUSED a self-conscious look on O'lyn. She was frightened over the reason she needed Mech's counsel and she was hesitant to let anyone else in on her secret. Truth be told, she'd gone to Mech because she knew how to be discreet. The last thing she needed was O'lyn getting involved in her nightmare. She stretched to make herself comfortable in the plastic beach chair Mech offered and finally gave up. O'lyn wasn't going anywhere.

"I need to disappear." She heard O'lyn suck in a breath and ignored it.

Mech, at least, seemed less concerned over her statement. Instead, she filled a shot glass full of 151 and shoved it at her. "Don't we all."

Veronica swallowed, not wanting to share more of the story. She considered pushing the shot away, and then elected to take it. Feeling a little braver after she swallowed the fiery liquid, she went on. "Listen, it's because..."

Mech held up a hand. "Trust me, if there's something that makes you need to disappear, the less people you share it with, the better." Veronica took another shot Mech offered gratefully; relieved she wouldn't have to share her nightmare story. "I'm assuming you're looking for credentials?"

Veronica tilted her head quizzically as she coughed over the 151. "Credentials?"

Mech let out a sigh. "You are not cut out for a life of crime." She took her own shot and went on. "Credentials. Passport, driver's license. All that jazz."

Veronica nodded.

Mech stretched and stood. "Pookie, we got a job."

Veronica spun around as a short nerdy boy appeared out of nowhere behind them. He clutched a hookah in his hand and brought the distinct smell of marijuana with him. "What's up?"

"We are in need of your artistic abilities."

"Dig it." He took a hit off his bong. "Passport and driver's license? The whole shebang?"

"The whole shebang, times two. We need a male and a female."

Veronica put up a hand. "I only need one." She gestured to O'lyn. "He's not coming with me."

Mech eyed O'lyn. "Shame." She met Veronica's eyes again. "Regardless, they're both for you."

Veronica was confused.

"You clear customs as a male. People are less likely to look at you if they're looking for the wrong gender." She gave a nod to Pookie who went off to begin his work. "You arrive in Costa Rica a female. It's like you never existed at all." She gave another wink. "Trust me; if you're looking to disappear, you've come to the right girl. According to the IRS, I died four years ago!"

Veronica took another deep breath, and another, and another. Soon, she was gasping. Somewhere, she heard someone say she was having a panic attack. She vaguely felt O'lyn press a hand into her lower back. A bag was shoved over her face and she breathed into it gratefully, the sound of crumpling paper finally drowning out the sound of the electric carving knife.

"That's right," A hand continued rubbing small circles into her back. "You're doing good. You're doing real good. Just keep breathing." The world around her started to come back into focus and she could feel O'lyn's lips brushing against her ear. She felt a small tremor of excitement at his closeness that she tried to shake away. Developing a crush was the last thing she needed. His hand continued to rub her back in small circles, relaxing her. She felt safe. For the first time since she found out her husband was a murderer, she felt safe.

"Thanks," She gasped as she sat back up again. "I'm sorry. Just... everything got to be too much."

O'lyn watched Veronica's pretty face in concern. She was white as a sheet and her eyes were tight. He could tell she was trying to be brave, but was bone tired and terrified. "It's okay." He caught her chin, tilting her face towards his. "I'll never let anyone hurt you, again ok?"

Veronica nodded and continued breathing into her paper bag. He could feel Mech's red-rimmed eyes burning into the side of his face. But this time, when he looked up, her expression wasn't filled with skepticism or suspicion. Instead, it looked like something akin to amused admiration. She waited until Veronica was under control before she spoke again.

"Do I need to do something besides getting you tickets?"

Veronica shook her head in confusion, clutching the paper bag in her hand. "What?"

"Are you in more trouble than disappearing can help?"

Veronica shook her head again. "No, I don't think so." Her face took on a stubborn set. "No, I'm sure. But I need a fake passport. Not tickets to anything."

"Tickets are fake passports. If you're going to embark on a criminal life, you could at least try to learn the lingo," Mech admonished her. "They'll be ready in two days." She caught Veronica's horrified look and gave a sad smile. "Sorry; if I could do it sooner, I would. But that's just how long it takes for Pook to make credentials that can fool a government official." She gestured towards the door. "Of course, you're welcome to stay here until that time."

Both O'lyn and Veronica watched as a rat the size of an overweight kitty skittered across the floor. Veronica gave a tense smile.

"I'm sure we'll be fine." She let out another deep breath along with another clutch of her brown paper bag. "What do I owe you?"

Mech shook her head. "No charge."

"Mech," Veronica looked at her in shock. "I insist."

Mech shook her head. "Nope, I owed you a solid."

"I gave you a three-block ride!" Veronica raised her head off O'lyn's shoulder and he watched her with amusement. "That is not worth ten thousand dollars' worth of forged credentials!"

Mech quirked her lips. "So you haven't forgotten everything I told you?" She let out a sigh. "Favors are worth whatever I decide they're worth." She pulled a business card out of her wallet. "I will see you in two days."

Veronica took the business card and stopped arguing. No one ever won an argument with Mech, and no one ever would. She had no illusions that she would be the first. "Fine, but I'm giving to charity in your name."

"Do what you feel, pretty Veronica." Mech winked again. "Just don't forget to come back if you need me."

O'lyn held Veronica carefully as she climbed into the passenger side of his jeep. The trip to the dilapidated bar had taken a lot out of her. The whole day had taken a lot out of her, and she was starting to look drained. He brushed her hair out of her face and buckled her in, feeling oddly protective.

"Where to now?"

"There's a motel down the street that will let me pay in cash. You can drop me there."

O'lyn's hands tightened on the steering wheel. "I'm not leaving you alone."

Veronica let out another sigh. "Listen, O'lyn, whatever you did to me in high school, you've completely made up for it after this crazy night." She pressed her face against the glass of his passenger side window as she absently wondered what her new life in Costa Rica would be like. "Just drop me off and move on. Trust me; you want no part of my crazy life."

O'lyn's grip got even harder. "Until you've actually remembered what I did to you, and until you've actually punched me in the face for what I did to you, I consider my debt unpaid and I'm staying with you until you do." He caught her tiny hand just as it was flying at his face. It was like being attacked with butterfly wings.

O'lyn gave her a stern look. "First, that was adorable. Remind me to teach you how to throw a decent punch later." He pushed her hand back onto her knee. "Second, the punch in the face doesn't count if you don't remember me." He flicked on his turn signal. "And third, when you do decide to punch me in the face, please don't do it while I'm driving." He could feel Veronica seething from the passenger seat and had to hold in a chuckle. She was cute when she was mad.

Finally, she calmed down. "So where are we going?"

"I'm getting us a room at a place that doesn't rent by the hour."

He could practically feel the tension pouring off of her. "I'm married."

"I know." He already decided they were going to discuss that situation further as soon as he got them settled in a room. Whatever she was running from, her husband was at the dead center. There was no way he was getting his hands back on her. "You're safe with me, okay?"

Veronica   felt his hand drop to her knee, but she had no desire to push it away. If his only ulterior motive was forgiveness for a crime she couldn't remember, then she was fine with that. All she cared about was that when he told her she was safe, she believed him

"She was spotted near Tatemville."

Clark sucked in a strangled breath. "Please tell me you're joking."

De 'Carlo shook his head sadly. "She was seen there with a man who matches the description of your pool cleaner. We think he gave her a ride."

"Into Tatemville?" Clark slammed his hands down on the table. "That's one of the most dangerous part of Savannah!"

"She wasn't there long. Only for a meet with the Jiven's sister."

"The Jiven's crew?" The suggestion did nothing to soothe him. Mechico Jivens was small-time, but vicious. He knew Veronica had a sort of friendship with her, but he'd chosen to discourage it. Mechico Jivens, who Veronica called Mech, was rumored to be more than a little unbalanced. He thought of his fragile little Veronica, terrified by what she had seen, racing along for any kind of help she could get.

"She was in and out in less than twenty minutes. With the pool cleaner."

Clark clenched his fists. "I want her returned to me. I want her returned to me unharmed and I want the pool cleaner dead for taking her." He shot an icy cold look to his second in command. "Do you understand?"

De 'Carlo nodded wordlessly and moved on to do his master's bidding. It was going to be an interesting week.

CHAPTER FOUR

"Was he abusive?" O'lyn rolled onto his side to appraise Veronica's response. They were staying in a mid-range, family-focused hotel chain in a much less scary part of the city than Tatemville. He'd gotten them a room with two double beds. Veronica wanted separate rooms at first, but O'lyn talked her out of it. He wanted her to stay close.

Veronica lay on her own bed, her eyes on the ceiling. She sighed. "No."

She shook her head negatively. "He could be a little intense, but he never hit me or anything."

"But you're changing your identity and fleeing the country to avoid him?"

Veronica rolled onto her side and focused her gaze on O'lyn. "Listen, that part, Mech said was right about. The less people who know, the better."

O'lyn folded his arm behind his head and decided to let the issue drop for a while. He would get it out of her eventually. Instead, he went for a subject change. "How does someone like you get tangled up with someone like Mech, anyway?"

Veronica smiled at the memory. "I met her about three years ago. I was turned around looking for a little antique shop, when I saw her running from a gang of boys." Veronica snorted. "It was kind of surreal. I slammed on my brakes and let her in the passenger seat. I'm not even sure why I did."

"Please tell me you're making this up?" O'lyn was leaning forward with interest.

Veronica shook her head negatively. "Nope. Turns out, she was having one of her 'episodes'. She hustled the young gang bangers out of all their money shooting craps in the alley."

"One of her episodes?"

"Yeah," Veronica rolled onto her back. "She's insane."

O'lyn shot to a seated position. "Literally?"

"Bipolar."

He turned towards Veronica, his face serious. "And you're going to her for help?" He shot up from the bed. "Jesus, Roni! How much trouble are you in you're going to a crazy person for help?"

Veronica crossed her arms over her chest and refused to look at O'lyn. "She's not always crazy. Just sometimes. Most of the time, she's normal." Her brow wrinkled. "Well, not really normal, but as normal as she can get."

O'lyn started pacing the room. "How do you know she's even going to come through? How do you know she can help you and get you out of the country?" He sat again, this time, on Veronica's bed and she leaned up on her elbows to see him.

"Because of who she is. Her full name is Mechico Jivens. Maybe you've heard of the Rickey Jivens Gang, she's done things like this before. All the time. It's what she does." Veronica lay back down. "Making a couple of ID cards for me is nothing."

O'lyn leaned towards her again, trying to get her to look at him. "Veronica, what kind of trouble, are you in? You're getting fake ID's so you can leave the country. You're consorting with criminals?"

"Says the guy who ran over my mailbox and drove away. That's a federal offense, you know." Veronica snorted.

"I didn't run over your mailbox!" He grabbed Veronica by the upper arms and gave her a rough shake. "Do you have any idea how stupid you're being?"

Veronica's eyes flashed with anger. "I'm not stupid." She shoved her way back. "Yeah, I might not be the smartest person in the world, but I'm not a fucking idiot."

O'lyn sighed and shook his head. "That's not what I meant, Veronica." He gave her shoulders a squeeze. "I just don't think you're thinking clearly." He released her and turned so he was seated next to her, his head pressed against the headboard of the bed. "Have you thought that maybe if you told someone, they might have other ideas?"

. "I can't tell anyone. They could get hurt, too." Veronica said, shaking her head.

"I'll never tell anyone. No one ever needs to know that I know." When she stayed silent, he went on. "Anyway, if anyone was watching, they're going to think I know, regardless. Think about it. You left in my jeep, after your housekeeper saw you talking to me. It won't take long for anyone to find out who I am."

Veronica let out a gasp and her eyes suddenly clouded with tears. "I didn't even think of that. Oh, God, O'lyn, I'm so sorry." She sprung out of the bed. "I have to get out of here. I'll go back to Mech. O'lyn, you need to leave town. You need to leave town tonight."

Her eyes were racing around the room, searching for things that belonged to her. Then she remembered; she had nothing. She made a dash towards the motel room door and hadn't even made it a foot before O'lyn's arm was snaking around her waist.

"I'm assuming that means you remember what happened in high school, then?" O'lyn muttered against her ear as he pulled her back against his broad chest.

"What the hell are you talking about? Let me go!" She struggled to break free, but his grip was like iron.

"That was the deal. You remember what happened, you forgive me for it, and I let you go. Until then, you're not going anywhere."

"Damn it O'lyn!" She struggled in his grip until she was facing him. She pulled back a hand to hit him and he caught it before her wild punch connected.

"I really need to teach you how to punch."

Veronica glared at him with hate in her eyes. She lifted a dainty foot while he focused on her face, still looking amused, and slammed it down on his instep as hard as she could.

"Ow, Fuck!" O'lyn yelped as he released her. "Well, at least you know how to do that right." He plopped down on the edge of the bed and began rubbing his foot.

"This is bigger than high school, O'lyn. This is bigger than a couple of insults and fat jokes. This is the kind of big no one can help me with."

O'lyn glared at his foot as he peeled off his sock. A bruise was already starting to form. "Well, maybe they could, if you would tell them what's going on."

Veronica threw her hands up in the air. "Fine, you want to know, O'lyn?" Her heart was pounding and when she managed to push the words out, they came out like a burst of gunfire. "My husband is a drug dealing monster and when he finds me, he's going to kill me." She threw a wild gesture at O'lyn, "And probably anybody I'm with."

Then she passed out.

When Veronica awoke, she was staring at an eggshell-white motel room ceiling. There was a cold cloth on her neck and someone was talking to her in a low, soothing voice. She blinked once, blinked again and tried to focus.

"Welcome back." O'lyn started rubbing her forehead with the cloth and she looked up at him stupidly. "So how did you lose the weight?"

Her brown eyebrows crumpled in confusion. "What?"

"The weight." O'lyn reached over to an ice bucket and dipped the cloth in the water again. He squeezed it out and put it back on her forehead. "You've dropped at least eighty pounds. How did you do it?"

Veronica sat up, pulling the cloth from her forehead. "Weight Watchers." She handed the cloth back to O'lyn. "You're not going to ask about my husband being a monster?"

O'lyn shook his head. "Nope." He dropped the cloth back in the ice bucket. "The way I see it, you've already been through enough. Truth be told, I already kind of figured out the whole 'drug dealing monster' angle anyway."

"Really? How?"

"Well," O'lyn turned and picked up the ice bucket to dump it in the sink in the bathroom. "You live in a gigantic house in Savannah with a wealthy possibly Spanish man who has no definable career."

Veronica flopped back against the pillows. "I am an idiot."

O'lyn smirked as he placed the towel back into the ice bucket. "No you're not."

"Really?" Veronica glared at him skeptically. "Then why am I the only person on the planet who apparently had no idea that my husband was a criminal? He was right. I am an idiot."

O'lyn sat on the bed next to Veronica.

"Again, no you're not. You're very smart." He smiled. "You're just a very sweet woman who only expects the best from people. Also, if he was calling you an idiot, then I'm glad you left him. No one should treat you like that."

Veronica's face heated up and she was surprised to find tears threatening to release from behind her eyelids. "Why are you being so nice to me?"

O'lyn stood and let out a sigh. "Because you're nice. You've always been nice. Even in high school, when most people were complete jerks to you, you were still nice. I just think you deserve someone being nice to you for a change." O'lyn crossed his arms over his chest. "I made a mistake with you before. I really hurt you, even if you don't remember it. The way I see it, this is karma. Karma brought me here for a reason and that reason is to help you." O'lyn's serious eyes met hers. "I won't force you to stay here if you don't want to. If you want to take off into the night, I wouldn't blame you. But if you do decide to stay, then know that I'm here and I'm not going to let anyone hurt you. Okay?"

Veronica nodded. She couldn't speak over the lump in her throat and she didn't trust herself to, anyway.

"Now let's talk about something else." O'lyn was uncomfortable with tears. "Something that doesn't make you get choked up every five seconds." He plopped back down on the bed next to her. "How'd you do all this?" He gestured in her direction.

"Do all what?"

"Go from angst-filled chubby teen to smokin' hot supermodel."

For the first time in hours, Veronica let out a genuine laugh. "My mom had an insurance policy. After she died, I got this fixed." Veronica gestured at her nose. "While I was recovering from the nose job, I lost my appetite and fourteen pounds. I decided to just go with it and kept dieting." Veronica leaned back on the pillows. "My family never had much money. We had to rely on non-perishable, starch-filled food to keep us fed." She gave O'lyn a knowing look. "When you're eating mac and cheese four times a week, it's hard to lose weight. When my mom passed, she left an insurance policy that paid out fifty thousand dollars. After I paid her doctors' bills, there was still thirty five left. It was more money than I'd ever seen in my life."

O'lyn stretched out on the bed beside her and Veronica stiffened. "Relax, I know you're married. I just want to listen and lay down at the same time. I won't try anything."

Veronica nodded, even though she found herself oddly disappointed. "Anyway, with so much money, I decided that I could move to anywhere I wanted to go. I picked Savannah. Being from New Orleans, I always wanted to stay near the water. I got my nose fixed and lost the weight. I was working as a bartender when a guy there offered me a job in the VIP room of his club. It was a great opportunity, because I was taking classes during the day." Veronica let out a nostalgic sigh. "I was going to be a veterinarian."

O'lyn leaned up off the pillows. "You worked in the animal shelter in high school." He thought back to the way Veronica's eyes would light up when she talked about the animals there.

Veronica nodded. "I've always loved animals. They're a lot easier to figure out than people." She smiled ruefully. "Anyway, it was working out well for me. I only had to work a few hours a week and I could spend the rest of my time studying. Then one night, some really rich guy came in. Instead of wanting me to wait on him, he wanted me to sit at his table. So I did."

"I'm assuming the really rich guy is now your husband?"

Veronica nodded. "I was really nervous at first. I kept spilling things and apologizing. Clark was surrounded by all these beautiful girls and I didn't know how to act around him." She shook her head. "He told me I was charming and he invited me out to dinner. Two months later, we were married. I always wondered what he saw in me."

"What do you mean?"

"He could have had anyone he wanted. Instead, he chose me." Veronica's expression turned bitter. "Turns out, I was just some beautiful idiot. All he wanted was pretty babies."

"You're not a beautiful idiot." O'lyn informed her firmly. "Well, you're beautiful, don't get me wrong. But you're not stupid, so please stop saying that."

"How do you know?"

"What?"

Veronica leaned up on her elbow and stared at him intently. "How do you know I'm not stupid? You barely know me."

O'lyn laughed. "Well, you're not stupid, but you have a terrible memory." He took in Veronica's questioning look. "You tutored me in biology for the last six months of my senior year. If it wasn't for you, I wouldn't have graduated."

Then it came back. Veronica remembered high school. A handsome dark-eyed boy she'd had a crush on. She'd been a year behind him in school, but Coach Thomas, her Advanced Biology teacher, begged her anyway.

"He's going to fail without you, Veronica."

"Damn it, Coach T, I'm a doctor, not a miracle worker!" They'd both laughed over her newly found memory and she'd agreed, because she liked

Coach Thomas and because O'lyn was right. She was nice.

She'd met him every day after school in the science lab. Thirty minutes every day of her explaining the finer points of biology and going over his homework with him. At first, he'd been angry and sullen over being forced to hang out with the fat girl in class when he could have been partying with his popular friends. But she'd always been nice. Over time, she thought they had become friends. They laughed together. They made jokes together. She developed a little crush on him, but knew it was hopeless. He was the handsome, popular football quarterback. She was the dumpy intellectual. It was such a fucking cliché.

Then came that day in the cafeteria. It was right after he passed his final exam and was about to graduate; thanks to her. He'd come up to her with a beautifully wrapped pink box.

"Veronica," He'd looked nervous and she'd wondered why. He'd already passed all his tests.

"Yeah?"

His friends were around him. She didn't know why; she only knew O'lyn was acting weird.

"I wanted to ask you a question?"

Veronica had nervously reached for her backpack. "Is it about biology, because I don't have my..."

O'lyn cut her off. "No. It's about prom."

"Prom?" Prom had been her fantasy. She'd never allowed herself to hope. The fat girl didn't get the guy, no matter how many times fantasized about it. No way was O'lyn Williams, the king of Wayne Co. High, asking her to prom.

"I want you to come with me."

Her heart had stopped. Her eyes had filled with joy. O'lyn Williams was asking her to prom. "I...I'd love to O'lyn." Her voice had cracked with emotions. She'd never been so happy.

O'lyn had cleared his throat. "Good, because I got something for you to wear."

Veronica gasped. In all her fantasies, she never expected it to go this far. She always pictured herself picking out her own dress, magically dropping five sizes and dazzling O'lyn in the doorway of her mother's two-bedroom trailer. She rushed to open the box, plopping it on the lunch table. The lunchroom had gone still in anticipation. All her dreams were coming true. Then, after ripping off the pretty pink paper, she was dashed back to reality. She opened the box.

Inside was a paper bag with two dark, black eyeholes cut out.

O'lyn's mocking voice echoed in her ears. "Because the only way I'd ever go anywhere with you is with a bag on your head."

Veronica's ears started to ring and she felt her face burning red. All she could hear was the cruel laughter of everyone in the senior class; their mocking looks intensified O'lyn's insult. Her eyes filled with tears and she raced out of the lunchroom with their laughter following her. Echoing... Echoing louder than a carving knife. Echoing in a way that makes you take the first available man that makes you feel beautiful. Echoing in a way that messes you up for life. Echoing in a way that makes you black out the bad parts, because when the cruelest joke was played, your mother was already dying of cancer and you couldn't handle anything else.

Veronica sucked in a gasp as she was dragged back to the present. O'lyn, the same O'lyn from high school, watching her with eyes filled with guilt. It was guilt he deserved. Veronica pulled her elbow back. She untucked her thumb. She shoved her fist out again, directly at O'lyn's nose. She threw the punch with all the weight in her body. And she felt the satisfaction as she felt it connect.

It was wonderful.

"Fuck you!" Veronica screamed as she pulled up from the bed. All of O'lyn's pretty words were forgotten. All she could remember was the humiliation in the cafeteria. Well, she wasn't that fat little girl anymore. She was beautiful and she would never deal with his taunts gain. "Fuck you."

She didn't even remember running. She could feel the door closing behind her, slamming behind her. She could hear his desperate plea.

"Veronica, come back!"

But she was never coming back. She was never coming back because

she was never going to be the girl she had been before. O'lyn was right. She was nice.

As far as she was concerned, nice was fucking overrated!

She hadn't even made it to the parking lot when she realized she had no idea where to go. Mech had offered to let her stay at the Brake Pad, but Veronica knew if Clark found her there, Mech wouldn't just turn her over. She'd probably start a war. Even seriously outnumbered, the Jivens crew would never go down without a fight. It was just how they were built.

She didn't want anyone to get hurt because of her. Well, except maybe O'lyn...and Clark. And she probably wouldn't mind if De 'Carlo were to suffer an injury or two.

Veronica looked around uncertainly. They were in a main area of Savannah. There were plenty of other motels, but she didn't have a dime on her. All she had was a passbook to her savings account, completely useless until the banks were open in the morning.

She focused her gaze at the bright lights of the strip, alive with music and bars that catered to tourists. With no destination in mind, she began walking towards them. She had no idea what she was going to do, but she would think of something. She had to.

As always, she was on her own.

CHAPTER

FIVE

O'LYN STARED IN THE MIRROR, flinching in pain as he put his nose back in the right position. Veronica's wild attack had packed a powerful hit. He decided he no longer needed to teach her how to punch.

O'lyn sighed, wondering what to do. She'd obviously remembered who he was and there was no way she wanted anything to do with him. He was afraid to leave her alone. She was fragile. She was sweet and she definitely didn't deserve the life she'd been given.

"Fuck," O'lyn muttered as he plopped down on the bed, holding a cold cloth to his nose to reduce the swelling. The punch didn't bother him the way her expression had. Those sad, grey eyes, looking lost, betrayed. He'd betrayed her and he'd never gotten over it. Apparently, she hadn't, either.

Now, she was on the run from a man trying to kill her and she didn't have any of the necessary equipment to take on the fight. O'lyn wondered if she'd go back to Mech, but he doubted it. She wouldn't want her friend to get hurt.

He wanted to go after her when she ran out of the room. He started to follow her, but stopped, realizing he was the last person she wanted. He still wanted to go find her, dragging her back to the room and keeping her safe, even if she didn't want him to. But he thought logically. She was scared enough. Upset enough. He didn't want to bother her further.

"But if she doesn't know I'm there." O'lyn stood up and looked in the mirror. He'd have a bruise in the morning and a slightly crooked nose in the future, but he looked ok enough to go out in public. He'd follow her. If she needed him, he'd be there. If not, she'd never know he was there. O'lyn stood, grabbing his keys.

She couldn't have gotten too far on foot.

Veronica nervously pulled on the door. She picked the quietest bar she could find. She'd hoped she'd be able to at least get off the street, hide for a while. She flinched a little as she realized the place was filled with college kids. Veronica ducked her head and pulled off her hood as she tried to sneak her way to the bathroom. Maybe she could hide out in one of the stalls for the evening.

"Wow, hello."

Veronica ducked her head a little harder, hoping someone hadn't recognized her. She focused her eyes on the bathroom door, where the painted lady adorned a sombrero and 'damas' Spanish for ladies. "Wait!"

Veronica gasped and took a step back as her way was blocked by a big freckled man, who was barely more than a boy, bouncing in front of her like an exuberant puppy. "What?" She glared at him and he gave her a dopey smile.

"Are you here with someone?" He was tall, wearing bright orange shirt indicating he was from Savannah State University. His smile was wide and his eyes were unfocused. He'd clearly had one too many drinks.

"I just needed to use the bathroom." She shoved her way past, hoping she wasn't looking at a drunken confrontation already. He moved out of her way easily and gave her a good natured smile as he did.

"Weird. Don't you guys usually go in packs?"

"What?"

"Girls. I thought you all went to the bathroom in groups?" He swayed awkwardly and Veronica reached out a hand to steady him. "Thanks."

"No problem." Veronica watched his face. It was open and honest, and a little ditzy. He seemed to be the harmless type. "You ok?"

He nodded drunkenly. "I cele...celebr...celebretating." He let out a drunken hiccup. "I'm twenty-one."

Veronica smiled as she remembered her own 21st birthday, which ended with her drunkenly vomiting in the parking lot outside a local club. "Congratulations." She smiled at him and started to walk by again.

He reached out and caught her elbow. Gently; not enough to cause her alarm. "Me and my friends have a table, if you need somewhere to hang out."

Veronica considered her options. She could hide out in a bathroom stall or she could at least have a warm seat at a table around a group of people. Being around people felt safer to her. "I changed my mind about the bathroom. Where are you guys?"

The drunken 21-year-old smiled happily and caught her by the hand, leading her back to a table where four other guys around his age sat. Everyone in the group smiled as she approached. Veronica sat with the group and soon found herself immersed in their conversation as if she'd known them for years instead of mere minutes. After downing a few lemon drop martinis, one of the young boys challenged her to enter the wet t-shirt contest.

O'lyn was pretty sure his jaw had dropped so hard it had actually unhinged when he'd walked into Tailgate, a small sports bar. It had been the last place he decided to look for Veronica, after going to every bar in town and coming up empty.

He'd found her. He was supposed to stay hidden, but he was frozen to the floor in shock. Veronica was standing center stage and accepting a prize of $500 after winning a wet t-shirt contest. She was wearing a white t-shirt with the bar name, "Tailgate" draped over her left breast and the shirt was near invisible after being sprayed down with a water bottle. People were screaming for her like she was a rock star.

She was a rock star. O'lyn felt his mouth go a little dry as he stared at the girl he'd known since high school. She was perfect. She was jumping up and down and making every guy in the bar swoon as she waved her prize around. His eyes locked on her bouncing breasts, hypnotizing him with the thought of what it would feel like to hold between his own lips.

"Veronica?" Her name came out like a croak.

Veronica finally spotted him and her eyes widened. She gave him a happy smile and jumped down from the stage, causing her chest to jiggle in a way that made the MC for the contest immediately propose. "O'lyn!"

O'lyn let out another gasp as she flung herself into his arms, soaking the front of his shirt. He didn't care. She felt incredible. He took advantage of her drunken moment and gave her a squeeze. "Oh my God!" She shrieked in his ear. "I'm having so much fun."

A dark-haired man with a beautiful brunette draped over him wandered past. "You are one lucky bastard."

The pretty brunette on his arm gave an unfocused nod. "Don't be mad at her. I told her to do it. Her tits are perfect."

Veronica nodded. "The trick is growing up fat and losing a bunch of weight." Veronica shot him a drunken glare. "You wanna put a bag on my head now, fucker?" She slumped against him and O'lyn smiled. Veronica was definitely wasted.

"I never wanted to," he muttered in her ear. "But we'll talk about that when you're sober." He looked down at her tiny, drunken, soaking wet frame. "You want me to carry you?"

Veronica gave him a drunken nod and wrapped her arms around his neck. "The room won't stop spinning. Make it stop doing that."

"Okay," he lifted her easily. She was light and her curves made her fun to carry. "Five hundred dollars, huh?"

Veronica shook her head as it lolled against his shoulder. "Six hundred. That pretty girl bought my NOLO t-shirt." She raised her head and looked down at herself. "Only now, I don't have anything to wear and this one is all wet for some reason."

O'lyn chuckled. "You can have one of mine."

Veronica gave a drunken smile, looking mollified. "Okay."

O'lyn carried her out the door to his jeep and pulled open the passenger side door. "Has anyone ever told you you're adorable when you're drunk?"

Veronica shook her head as well as she could without making the jeep spin as O'lyn tucked her into the passenger seat and buckled her in. "Nope. I don't get drunk a lot." She slid her gaze over to him. "You think I'm adorable?"

O'lyn nodded as he gunned the engine. "Incredibly."

"You wanna have sex?"

O'lyn sucked in a breath and had to resist the urge to tackle her. "Very much." He gave his passenger, encased in a tight, white, wet t-shirt a thorough once over. "More than anything, to be honest. But I'm not going to."

Veronica pouted, managing to look even cuter. "Why not?"

O'lyn sighed, "Because you're drunk and you'll hate me in the morning."

"Oh O'lyn," Veronica laughed. "I already hate you! What does a little more hatred matter?" She snorted and left her head drift to the right so she could look out the window. "The very least you could do is get me off."

O'lyn felt like he had been punched in the stomach. "You hate me?"

Veronica snorted. "Why wouldn't I?" Her expression went bitter. "Get in my shoes for once. Your mother is dying. Your home is filled with nothing but the smell of death, the sound of death. The little noises she makes when the doctor is taking yet another bone sample. You know she's trying not to scream from the pain. She's doing it for you. But you want to scream for her and you can't. Dad is off somewhere playing a poker game, he could never win. You go to school and people treat you like a monster because you dare not to be perfect. You don't weight ninety-five pounds and you don't have a perfect button nose." Her eyes slid to him. "Then, you finally meet someone you trust. You start to gain feelings you've never felt. You spend thirty minutes a day with him and it's the best thirty minutes of your entirely miserable day." She straightened in her seat. "Then, the only person you trust humiliates you in front of the entire school for no more reason than you dared to have a crush on him." She rolled her eyes. "You wanna try that day for a change, O'lyn? Will that help with your selfish little guilt problem."

O'lyn's heart clenched and his hands tightened on the steering wheel. "Roni I …"

"You know why you feel guilty, O'lyn?" Veronica's voice was getting stronger and anger was making her buzz wear off. "Because you deserve to. I know your excuses and I know your reasons. Your popular friends were making fun of you. They were teasing you about your relationship with the fat girl. Instead of being brave, telling them to fuck off, you decided to destroy me." Veronica smirked. "Well the joke was on you, O'lyn. The joke was on you and now you're living it." She reached for the door handle as they pulled into the motel parking lot. She shoved her door open, damn near sober and fully ready to walk off into the night again. "Because I've always been brave and you don't even know what the word means." She slammed the door shut, feeling self-righteous and powerful. She stomped around the Jeep without hearing O'lyn's response, fully ready to go off on her own.

And walked right into De 'Carlo's arms.

O'lyn heard Veronica's harsh intake of breath and realized what happened. There was a black Town Car parked behind his jeep and he hadn't even noticed them pull up. He'd been too busy being berated by Veronica ...and a little heartbroken over the fact that she hated him.

A man who was easily twice his size and triples hers was wrapping his arms around her. He spoke, with just a hint of a Spanish accent, to a man behind him. "Take care of the pool boy. I'll get Mrs. Torres in the car."

"Pool boy?" O'lyn muttered. He watched as a smaller man raised a gun and trained it on him. O'lyn ducked just in time to avoid the bullet. He could hear Veronica shrieking as she struggled in the other man's grip. The man began to drag Veronica towards the back seat of the Town Car.

Another bullet shot off the pavement in front of him and O'lyn ducked down further. He could still hear Veronica's struggles. His fists tightened as Veronica let out a yelp of pain. O'lyn stood. He ignored the smaller man looking at him in frightened alarm and, instead, focused on the larger man, who was trying to shove Veronica into the backseat of their car.

O'lyn squared his chest and he ran. Just as the man was shoving her into the car, he tackled him with all the weight in his body. The man was forced to let go of Veronica.

"Veronica, run!" O'lyn yelled at her as he tackled the man to the ground. He didn't turn around to make sure she had done as he told her to. Instead, he began pummeling the larger man with his fists, his hands making a meaty thud every time they connected. O'lyn nailed him in the face and felt the blood spray his arm. He'd broken the bastard's nose. He threw another punch, nailing him in the eye socket, and another and another until the man stopped struggling. O'lyn stopped punching, realizing that the bastard was unconscious.

He stood. The smaller man was still holding a gun on him but had yet to fire a shot. He could see the fear in his eyes.

"Are you going to shoot me or not?" O'lyn took a menacing step towards him, aware of how grizzly he looked covered in blood. The man took a step back and dropped his gun, throwing his hands in the air in a gesture of surrender.

"That's what I thought. Where did she go?" The man pointed towards the back of the motel and O'lyn ran in that direction. He cut down the only alley behind it, making a sharp right at a chain-link fence. He cut down yet another ally, following the streetlights. For some reason, knew Veronica would have followed the streetlights when she ran. Finally, after running for what felt like hours, he stopped under the dim orange light of a parking lamp. He gasped to catch his breath and wiped off his forehead with his arm. As he was gasping for air, he heard a whisper behind him.

"O'lyn?"

O'lyn let out a gasp of relief and raced to where Veronica was crouched behind a dumpster, hiding and watching him with wide eyes. "Veronica, honey. I told you to run," he admonished her gently, at the same time feeling relieved he found her.

"I called Mech." Veronica pointed to the convenience store across the street. "I figured it was a sign when the guy let me use his phone."

O'lyn thought back to the psychopath he'd met earlier. "I don't know if bringing Mech into this is a good..."

O'lyn didn't get to finish his sentence. Just as he was about to, a Chevy Capris squealed to a stop in front of them. The passenger side window rolled down and a bleached blonde head popped out.

"Well, are you guys coming or not?"

Veronica's eyes widened as she realized what was in the passenger seat. "What is that?"

Mech snorted. She gave the animal's fuzzy head a pat. "Oh that's my baby, isn't she just adorable and only six months old." Mech smiled and turned her attention back on the road. "I named her Killer."

O'lyn focused on the animal, who was now glaring at him. "That is a mighty big dog!"

"Careful now, lover boy...she doesn't like men too much!"

O'lyn turned to Veronica. "This is the woman who is going to help you flee the country?" He turned back to the Rottweiler in the passenger seat in time to watch it bear his teeth in a menacing growl.

"Careful," Mech gave Killer's head another pat. "She gets very territorial." Mech waved her hand at them as she saw headlights approaching. "Get down."

O'lyn and Veronica didn't need to be told twice. They both ducked in the backseat as low as they could. "She's fucking insane." O'lyn hissed at

Veronica. They both held their breath as Mech slammed on the brakes, clearly having been cut off by someone. They heard Mech cuss and roll down the window.

"Evening Jivens." Veronica stiffened as De 'Carlo's voice filled the car. "What's got you out on this side of town so late at night?"

"What's it to you, Lurch?" Veronica had to hold in a giggle. De 'Carlo did look a little like a Latin Lurch.

De 'Carlo's voice was tight when he spoke again. "Look, I...What the fuck is that?" De 'Carlo had spotted Killer.

"Rottweiler."

Killer let out another low growl.

"I heard there were some Columbians hot to get their hands on you. It'd be quite easy to set up a little meeting with them, you know."

Mech sighed and O'lyn tensed. Would she turn them over to save her own ass? He tilted his head as Mech began to speak again.

"It would be a shame if a certain Punta got blown to hell when he was trying to set up a meet with a bunch of Columbians. You wanna talk to them about me; be my guest. We both know you'd never leave their place alive. You and the Columbians are like vinegar and water"

"You mean oil and water?"

"Nope, vinegar and water. Just like douche bags." Mech tapped her steering wheel impatiently. "Now can you get to your point and move your fucking car? I need to get this thing home before it shits all over my passenger seat."

De 'Carlo let out a defeated snort. "I need to know why Veronica Torres was at your bar tonight."

"How the fuck should I know?" Mech gestured to the Rotti. "I was out walking this thing."

"That wouldn't take all night."

"Have you ever tried walking this big ass dog?" Mech let out a laugh. "Listen, my guess would be that Veronica was at the bar to see my brother."

"Your brother?"

"Yeah, Mooki." Mech stretched in her seat. "He's an artist. Veronica asked him to do a picture of her a few weeks back."

De 'Carlo sounded confused. "A picture."

"Yup, a portrait. It's supposed to be a gift for her husband."

"So Veronica Torres was at your bar to check on a painting she was having done?"

"That would be my guess." Mech started to roll up her window. "Or she was getting her money back for it. I don't think Mooki even started it, yet. Now if you'll excuse me."

De 'Carlo sighed and stepped back from the car. "Fine, but if you hear anything," De 'Carlo shoved a slip of paper at Mech, "contact me. There's a reward out."

Mech looked at the slip of paper. "A reward, you say? Well, we both know how much I love money." Then, to Veronica's surprise, De 'Carlo laughed and walked away from the window. A few seconds later, Mech was driving again. Both Veronica and O'lyn waited.

"All clear."

They both popped up in the backseat, breathing hard.

"I take back what I said;" O'lyn informed Mech. "You're not insane. You're a genius. Veronica was worried. "Won't they check with Mooki?"

"Nope," Mech shook her head. "Lurch is just going to assume you went to Mooki to get your money back so you'd have an escape stash. The Jivens crew is officially not related to your disappearance and I have dried up their only lead." Mech smiled proudly. "I'm a world-class liar. So where to? I have to get Killer some dinner."

"Well, we wouldn't want him to miss a meal." O'lyn turned to Veronica. "Where are we going?"

Veronica frowned and glared at O'lyn. "I'm still mad at you. I don't care where you go. I'm going with Mech."

"Awesome, we can have a sleepover, braid each other's hair and talk about boys and stuff." Killer let out a wail. "Fine, you can come, too."

Killer snorted.

"Veronica ..." O'lyn tried to reach for her hand and she yanked it away, glaring out of the backseat window and refusing to meet his eye.

"Uh oh." Mech's slightly unbalanced gaze focused on the rearview. "We got company."

Veronica spun around in her seat. "Oh, god. It's De 'Carlo, isn't it?" She watched as a yellow Monte Carlo began approaching them at a high rate of speed.

Mech shook her head. "Nope, these fuckers are here for me." She met Veronica's questioning look. "The Columbians..." Mech slammed her foot down on the gas and the car shot forward.

"I was kind of in the middle of my own high-speed chase when you called me."

Veronica screamed as the Monte Carlo caught up to them and rammed into the rear bumper. Mech let out scorching stream of cuss words and jerked the wheel hard to the left. She reached out a hand and popped open the glove compartment. "Hey handsome, you're a wannabe soldier, right?"

"Yeah, how'd you..."

She tossed a gun back at him. "We'll discuss my amazing powers of observation later. For now, shoot them." Mech jerked the wheel harder and spun a U-turn in the middle of the road. The Monte Carlo slammed on its brakes and began to reverse, clearly not expecting a frontal assault.

O'lyn looked at the gun in his hand and then looked to Veronica's terrified face as she clutched on the rear of the passenger seat to avoid being tossed around like a rag doll. Without another thought, he slammed the butt of the gun into the window, shattering the glass. Then, he pushed his body halfway out and began firing. His first shot took out the windshield and the Monte Carlo's tires squealed as it continued its backwards race to get away from Mech's approaching Capris.

"Go for the tires," Mech yelled over Killers barking and growling.

O'lyn listened. He dropped the site on the glock low to the ground, led the car slightly and fired. He watched in satisfaction as the front driver's side tire exploded and the Monte Carlo began rocking out of control. He fired again and took out a rear tire. The Monte Carlo began to slip. Sparks shot up from the pavement as the rims of the exploded tires scraped the road. The Monte Carlo spun to the right and crashed into a telephone pole, coming to a jarring stop.

Mech let out a whoop of joy from the front seat as she raced past the wreckage. "Nicely done, Jarhead. You do this often?"

O'lyn let out a gasp and stared at the gun in his hand. "Nope, I can honestly say that this is my first high-speed chase."

Mech smiled and took the gun back, reducing her speed to normal now that the threat was passed. "Well, you'll get used to it. Welcome to Savannah."

"Thanks." O'lyn shook his head. "So how'd you know?"

"The wannabe soldier thing? Your haircut is terrible, you're built like a brick shithouse and you called me ma'am. You wanted to be a military man at some point. You learned all the protocol. The only thing that kept you back was your color blindness." Mech smirked.

O'lyn sat back, stunned. "You noticed all that?"

Mech winked. "I'm not just crazy; I'm also a genius." Mech turned her focus to Veronica. "Is she gonna hyperventilate again? I'm out of bags."

O'lyn realized Veronica hadn't spoken in a while and he turned to her. She was watching him with open astonishment. "How'd you do that?"

"Do what?"

"Shoot out their tires like that?"

O'lyn gestured to Mech. "Training for the military, like Mech said. I did weekend classes before enlistment, part of a military prep class. Then I failed the vision test and that was that."

"How'd you get away from De 'Carlo?"

"I kicked his ass." O'lyn's brow crumpled in confusion. "How do you think?"

Mech let out a laugh from the front seat. "So you're the person who crushed De 'Carlo's nose? O'lyn, I got to tell you, I'm really starting to like you. His face looked even worse than yours. Not too many people can say that after a fight with De 'Carlo."

O'lyn smirked. "Actually, Veronica did this."

Mech burst out laughing, and weirdly, it sounded like Killer was laughing right along with her. When she finally calmed down, she started speaking again. "Listen guys, not that you two aren't truly entertaining, but me and Killer have some planning to do. I know a motel. Safe part of town, you can pay in cash, and its meth lab free. You want me to bring you there?"

"You did that for me?" Veronica still looked astonished. "Why?"

O'lyn sighed. "Because I like you. And I owe you. You were the only reason I graduated high school and I repaid that by betraying you. As far as I'm concerned, all the crazy shit that's happened since I met you is karma paying me back for that. So I'm going to help you, even if it means getting my ass kicked or getting bit by a pit..."

"Rotti," Mech corrected.

O'lyn caught Veronica's hand and gave it a squeeze. She didn't try to pull away. "I just want to help."

Veronica blinked slowly, nodded. "Okay," she finally decided. "Okay, you can help. Mech? Can you bring us?"

"You got it." Mech flicked on the directional and made a right turn to bring them to the 'meth lab free' motel.

CHAPTER SIX

"What the hell do you mean she got away?"

De 'Carlo sighed and nearly rubbed his eye, before he remembered how swollen it was. "The pool boy has an excellent left hook." He cleared his throat, nervous with his boss' silence. "I did track down Mech from the Jivens crew, though. "It doesn't look like the wops were too heavily involved. Mrs. Torres went there to get her money back for a painting she was having done for you."

Clark nearly hissed into the phone. "She returned one of my gifts to get money to run away from me?"

"That's what it sounds like."

"De 'Carlo, perhaps you didn't understand my wishes initially. I want my wife returned and I want the pool boy dead, great left hook or no. If you are unable to handle that, I will find somebody who can." Clark took a deep breath. "Unfortunately, that means I will have to terminate your employment. You understand what that means in this business, right?"

De 'Carlo swallowed, remembering a carving knife. "I understand."

"Good." Clark clenched the phone. "I'll expect her back no later than tomorrow evening, then. See that it happens." He hung up the phone without waiting for an answer.

"Bad news?" De 'Carlo glared at the driver of the Town Car, Marcus. He let out a sigh and placed the icepack back on his forehead.

"Nothing new, my boss is a dick."

Veronica winced at the same time O'lyn flinched as she placed and icepack on his nose. "I'm really sorry."

O'lyn held the icepack to his face and let a hand drift to Veronica's hip. "No worries. I deserved it."

Veronica shook her head. "No you didn't. Listen, that stuff I said, before De 'Carlo attacked us..."

"Was completely right." O'lyn pressed the icepack on his face harder, lying back against the pillows. "I was an idiot in high school. Believe it or not, I really liked you." O'lyn peeked out from under the icepack to watch Veronica's reaction. "I just didn't know what to do about it. When my friends started making fun of me, I got pissed and I took it out on you. My life was never the same after that day."

Veronica picked up the icepack to examine his eye. "What do you mean?"

O'lyn tried to not stare at her chest as he continued. "Bad luck started following me around." O'lyn thought back. "On prom night, the night I should have been with you, I took a thot named LaKisa, instead. She was so damn obnoxious; I just started drinking to avoid her talking."

"I remember LaKisa. Cheerleader, right?"

"Yeah," O'lyn nodded. "Anyway, we went to her brother's place, because he was over twenty-one and could buy beer. I got wasted and decided to be the big man by driving everyone home." O'lyn shook his head bitterly. "I didn't even make it out of the driveway before I backed into a tree. No major damage, but I tore my ACL in the accident. I lost my football scholarship."

"O'lyn, I'm so sorry."

O'lyn shook his head empathically. "Nope, I deserved it. I didn't deserve a football scholarship after what I did to you." He sat up straight in the bed and the icepack dropped off his face. "Instead, I tried to join the Army. Like Mech said, even they didn't want me. I'm color blind. Then, I traveled around for a bit. I tried to go back to college, but I couldn't afford it and I couldn't get financial aid. I've tried out for several AFL teams. Every time things started to go right, something would happen to make them all go bad again. After a while, I thought maybe it was the universe's way of getting back at me. Every time I thought something was going good, I'd just flash back to your sad, grey eyes and everything would turn to shit again. So, when I was driving by Savannah, I decided to drop in and see you, just to tell you I was sorry." O'lyn gave a rueful smile as a sudden thought occurred to him. "Are your eyes really grey, or am I wrong about that, too?"

Veronica smiled gently. "No, they're really grey."

O'lyn leaned closer and started to stroke her cheek. "I knew it. I knew I couldn't be wrong about that." He let out a nostalgic smile. "You always had the most beautiful eyes, even when the rest of you wasn't as beautiful."

"That's kind of a dick thing to say."

O'lyn shook his head, realizing he'd gone the wrong way. "Not like that. I mean, even though you weren't the prettiest girl in school, I liked you anyway. I liked you more than those other girls and I felt weird about liking you that way. So I got mad. Then I did that thing to you, and it destroyed me, in more ways than one. My life will never be right until I make up for that day."

Veronica pulled back in surprise. "Have you always felt this guilty?"

O'lyn nodded. "I came looking for you after school that day to apologize but you weren't anywhere to be found."

"Listen, O'lyn," Veronica sighed. "My entire life wasn't defined by that moment. I had good times and I had bad times. After a while, I forgot about you entirely and went on with

my life. I made my own decisions."
Veronica shook her head. "I'm sorry
you feel bad for the way my life is now,
but it's not your fault. Even if it was, I
wouldn't trade it."

"You wouldn't?"

"No." Veronica laughed as she
remembered her first few years in
Savannah. "I had fun. I made a lot of
great friends. I learned you can make
mistakes and reinvent yourself. I
learned that destiny isn't pre-
determined. You create it yourself. I
would have never had the bravery I
needed to walk away from the town we
grew up in if I thought there was
anything left for me there. Instead, I
did and I got to lead a pretty
interesting life." She caught O'lyn's
hand. "High school is only four years
of your life, O'lyn. It doesn't decide
who you are. You do."

O'lyn was looking at her oddly.
His eyes dropped to her mouth and
her forehead crinkled in confusion.

Suddenly, he lurched out and latched onto her, his lips meeting hers. She let out a little squeak at the start of the kiss, but as the warmth enveloped her, she wrapped her arms around his neck. She pressed her mouth to his, harder, and parted her lips, encouraging him in.

Suddenly, O'lyn pulled back. "I'm sorry. I don't know what I was thinking." O'lyn pushed away. "I know you're married. I just keep thinking you shouldn't be."

Veronica let out a gasp, still breathing heavy over their very brief kiss. "What do you mean?"

O'lyn sat next to her on the bed, still watching her lips. He was hesitant for a minute, but finally spoke. "You should have been mine."

"What?"

O'lyn shook his head. "It's so damn clear now. Your asshole husband should have never got his hands on you in the first place." O'lyn leaned in close to her ear. "You were supposed to be with me. It wasn't karma telling me to find you. It was fate."

"O'lyn, I..." Veronica let out as gasp as O'lyn embraced her, his mouth pushing down on hers insistently. For a second, she was frightened, but after a moment, she gave in. He was what she'd wanted all along, after all. She wrapped her arms around him and pulled him closer. She started pulling at his shirt. "You promised me a shirt."

O'lyn raised his mouth from hers for a second. "Did I?"

"I want this one."

O'lyn chuckled as she ripped the shirt from his body. "Ok." He sucked in a breath as her fingernails grazed his chest. "You want the pants, too?"

Veronica nodded and he moved his hands to oblige her.

Veronica awoke in a sweaty tangle of limbs. O'lyn's body was draped over hers, his arm wrapped around her waist in the same possessive way Clark always held her.

Veronica now knew the difference. O'lyn wanted to be with her. Clark thought of her as property.

She studied his sleeping, handsome face in the darkness. His arm reached out for her, even though she wasn't there. He snatched the pillow she'd been sleeping on, cuddling it close.

Blinking over the tears that were starting and walking across the room, she picked up. She had no choice. She hadn't missed the words that De 'Carlo had spoken.

"Take care of the pool boy."

Veronica shook her head. She knew enough of the underworld terminology to know that 'take care of' did not mean O'lyn was getting a bowl of hot soup and a warm blanket. O'lyn's guilt, his crazed belief in karma, would drive him to do anything for her, but she wasn't going to let that happen. Instead, she was going to make sure he was safe, even if it meant sacrificing herself in the process. Because she loved him. She had always loved him. It only took one night with him to remember how much.

She picked up the phone. She could endure Clark. She would live with her own night in the attic; accept the pain he would instill on her. After what she saw, it would only take a few hours, probably less. She was decidedly less oblivious to pain than Herman. She could live with a few hours of pain before she died, as long as he promised one thing. That he would leave the pool boy alone. She gave O'lyn a gentle glance as she put the phone to her ear. He would love again and he would find someone again. She could do that much for him, after everything he'd tried to do for her. She could do that one thing for him before she stopped breathing altogether. She was scared, but she would be brave. She would be brave for him, and someday, she would meet him in heaven.

Veronica flinched as her husband's gruff voice answered on the first ring. "Clark, I'm ready to come home...but I have a couple of conditions."

"You have no idea how pissed off Mr. Torres is."

Veronica rolled her eyes as De 'Carlo shoved her into the backseat of a Town Car. She'd accepted her fate, as long as O'lyn was safe. True to his word, Clark left O'lyn alone, on the condition that Veronica returned home immediately.

"I have a general idea." Veronica answered dryly. "I'm assuming it involves a carving knife." Veronica wasn't scared. Clark couldn't hurt her now. She was in love and she was keeping the man she loved safe. Nothing could hurt her. She was bulletproof.

De 'Carlo looked at her strangely in the rearview. "We'll see about that." Marcos was seated next to him and refused to meet her eyes.

She was dead. And she was strangely okay with that. She let her gaze drift as she was driven through the familiar orange blossom field she'd become accustomed to. The night was light, thanks to the full moon. As they left Savannah and headed to the suburbs of the county, the starlight grew. Veronica wondered if she would be able to see it from the attic window. She wasn't afraid. She was feeling strangely stoic about her impending death. As long as O'lyn was all right.

"We're home." De 'Carlo announced as he stopped the car. Veronica sighed. Her night of fantasies was over and the pain would begin soon. She didn't struggle as De 'Carlo dragged her out of the car. She didn't protest or fight. She wasn't even afraid as she saw Clark's silhouette appear in the doorway of the home she'd once loved. She was apathetic and ready for it all to be over.

"Veronica." Clark let out a breath and snatched her by the shoulders, studying her closely. "Look at me."

Veronica glared at Clark, trying to make sure her obvious hatred of him showed through. "What?"

Clark glared at her. "What do you mean what? Do you have any idea how worried I've been?"

"Whatever," Veronica shoved her way past him. "Let's get this over with."

"Get what over with?"

Veronica sighed. "The part where you murder me with a carving knife in our attic." She turned towards the stairs. "Let's get this party started. I don't have all night."

Clark shook his head. "Veronica, I would never do that to you." He moved to grab his young wife and she flinched away. "You've been nothing but loyal to me." He sighed as he dragged her against his chest. "I know what you saw was scary, but you need to believe me; I wouldn't do that to you."

Veronica tried to shove away, but Clark held tight. "Wait, you're not going to kill me?"

Clark let out a laugh. "Why would I do that?"

"Because of what I saw."

Clark gave her an indulgent smile. "And did you tell anyone what you saw?"

"Well, no but I thought..."

"That was your problem right there." Clark gave her a kiss on the forehead. "Thinking..." He gave her a gentle pat on the bottom to shove her up the stairs. "Go to bed. We'll talk about it in the morning."

Veronica shook her head in confusion, but continued her way up the stairs. So Clark wanted to kill her in the morning. Whatever. She was dead inside, already. Veronica sighed and went to bed like Clark told her to.

Clark watched as Veronica sullenly went up the stairs to their room. She seemed different now that she'd returned – agitated, angry and more than a little defiant. He shook his head. He would take care of whatever attitude problem Veronica had developed in the morning. For now, he had other things to deal with. He turned and focused his angry eyes on De 'Carlo. "Now get back to the motel and finish the pool boy off."

"You told Mrs. Torres…"

Clark nearly growled in frustration. "What I tell my wife is none of your business." He took an angry step towards De 'Carlo. "That pool boy took something that belongs to me. I do not take kindly to others touching my property." He shot a look up the stairs. "He also crushed my mailbox. That's two items I own that he damaged.

O'lyn's eyes widened as he walked into the Brake Pad. When he'd woken in the motel room and found a goodbye note from Veronica, he didn't waste time going to her house. Instead, he knew that he needed help of another kind. The kind of the criminal variety. He went back to see Mech, hoping she hadn't left town yet. She hadn't, but she obviously had a very busy night after she dropped them off. The bar had been a mess before but now it looked even worse.

Literally.

He noticed Killer and about twenty cages filled with small puppies ranging from Rottis to pits and poodles.

"Hey O'lyn."

O'lyn let out a laugh, unsure of where to begin. "I thought you were splitting town to hide from the Columbians."

Mech spun around and, as she did, the bird flew off her shoulders. "I was going to, but then I decided 'in for a penny, in for a pound' and went back to steal all their babies, instead." She gestured towards the bar. "Hence, the current state of my establishment. Can I get you anything? Beer, whisky?"

"Take a seat," she gestured towards the floor. "But mind the kitty"

O'lyn sprung off of the barstool as he saw what was sleeping on the floor less than a few feet away from him. "You stole a fucking tiger?"

"Well yeah," Mech held up a box. "Who did you think the frosted flakes were for?" She smiled at O'lyn's hesitation. "Relax. All the dangerous ones are drugged out of their minds. Pearl won't be waking up any time soon."

"You named the tiger Pearl."

"She's a lady tiger." Mech looked towards the door. "Speaking of ladies, where's Veronica?"

O'lyn shook his head as he slumped back down onto the barstool, man-eating lady tiger forgotten. "That's why I'm here." O'lyn yanked a piece of paper out of his back pocket. "She left this for me this morning."

Mech spread out the piece of paper on the bar in front of her and read Veronica's messy, cursive script out loud.

Dear Olyn,

Last night was wonderful. I really missed you and it was great to see you again. But being with you made me realize how much I love my husband. I know he's not the best person in the world, but he's been good to me and I think we can work it out. I'm going home. Please don't come looking for me.

I'm sorry for everything I got you involved in. It wasn't right to drag you into my problems. In any case, it might be a good idea if you leave Savannah.

Good luck with everything and I hope you have a wonderful life. You're a very good person, even if you don't think you are. In case you were wondering, your apology is accepted and I forgive you for everything.. including running over my mailbox.

Love,

Veronica

p.s. Thanks for the shirt

Mech looked back up at O'lyn as she finished. "So in general, you two did the dirty deed and Veronica had some morning-after regrets and went running back to her husband." She shoved the paper back at O'lyn. "I'm sorry, but if you're looking for relationship advice, I'm the last person in the world that can help. I broke up with my last boyfriend by stabbing him with a fork."

O'lyn shook his head as he took back the 'Dear John' letter. "She's lying."

"How do you know?"

O'lyn folded the paper as he shoved it in his back pocket. "In high school, I showed Veronica a note I forged from my parents for senior skip day. Veronica laughed and threw it out, and then she rewrote it for me. She told me my handwriting was 'too perfect' and that if you were going to tell a lie, it was best to write messy. That way, it looks like you didn't think about it too much." O'lyn shook his head. "Veronica's handwriting is usually perfect. I've seen it. It's like damn calligraphy."

"Yeah, she's got a bit of OCD."

"She thought I wouldn't remember her trick. She wanted to make the note look genuine, like she was just some spoiled rich wife going back to her husband after a weekend adventure." O'lyn's eyes darkened. "I know better. She was terrified of him."

Mech let out a humorous laugh. "Of course she was terrified. He's a drug lord, for god's sake."

"Veronica didn't know that."

Mech's eyes got wide. "She didn't?" Mech shoved her way around the bar. "Of fucking course she didn't. I wasn't here to tell her that when they got married." Mech smacked herself in the forehead. "I barely even knew they were dating. When I got back from hiding out after the bust on my brother, they were already married."

"Your brother? Who, Mooki?"

Mech gestured to the animals in the bar again. "This is an ongoing thing. I was distracted."

"With dog fighting?"

Mech snorted. "Please. There's no money in dog fighting. This is about diamond smuggling." Her eyes widened excitedly as she said the word 'diamond.'

"Diamond smuggling?" O'lyn spun around on his barstool as Mech walked across the bar. She reached for Killer and gave her an affectionate scratch on the neck, gently pulling off the collar.

Mech nodded. "I discovered it purely by accident. I was at the docks, doing a little business of my own, when I heard a little growl from behind. I dropped my business in the ocean. So I did the only reasonable thing anyone would do and stole the dog. I decided to disappear for a while afterwards because I wasn't sure if anyone saw me. So me and the dog are living it up in a beach shack in South Beach. I noticed the collar, and took it to a little pawn shop to get appraised. First I thought they were rhinestones you know. Turns out two of the stones were worth fifty thousand dollars."

Mech rolled her eyes. "I did some checking around. These dogs and that tiger are being shipped around the country to pet stores; the only thing is the stores are fronts. The dogs are being used to smuggle the diamonds in from Africa, Germany and China. Animals you see don't go through the same custom checks as humans do. And since each one is going to a different store in different areas, no one has caught on that the collars contain real jewels.

"So?" O'lyn was confused.

"So," Mech emphasized, "It's just a really clever way to smuggle conflict diamonds from Africa to America without anyone being the wiser." Mech laughed out loud. They're fragile, and tend to die when subjected to things like exams and x-rays. The smugglers collect their diamonds and no one is the wiser. Unfortunately, I was in the docks the same night a rare Azawakh was being shipped in. I was there with two diamonds, waiting to pay off some guys I know for a shipment of plastic explosives. The fucking thing startled me and I dropped my diamonds in the ocean." She gestured around the bar. "Every animal in here has conflict stones around their necks. Usually, when they get here, the assholes will just dispose of them or sell them on craigslist. I'm just procuring the stones and turning the animals over to people who will take care of them." Mech smiled as she petted Killer again. "Everybody wins."

"What does this have to do with Veronica?"

"Absolutely nothing." She smiled at O'lyn. "Sorry, I have a tendency to get distracted." She looked around at her bar now dog refuge. "But we might be able to use this to our advantage."

"How so?"

"You probably don't want to know." She reached in her back pocket for her keys. "Now help me get the tiger into the trunk of my car."

O'lyn sighed as he stood from his barstool. Sure, she was insane, but she was his only hope.

CHAPTER SEVEN

VERONICA GLARED ACROSS the breakfast table at her husband. Clark had yet to say anything to her about what she'd seen and what she knew. "Are we even going to talk about it?"

Clark gave her an indulgent look and returned to his sports page. "There is nothing to discuss Veronica.

You're home now. That's all that matters."

Veronica glared at him in confusion. "How can you say that? What I saw..."

"Was nothing more than a business matter and you don't need to worry your beautiful head about it."

Veronica glared again. "My beautiful idiot head, you mean."

Clark sighed and folded his paper, finally giving Veronica his full attention. "I am sorry you took offense at that. I will admit it was an ill-formed opinion. I was just trying to say that it is not your job in this household to think. It is your job to be beautiful and give me children. Stick to your strengths."

Veronica felt a wave of fury that she'd never felt before. "My strengths? Well, you're right about one thing. I'm great at baby making." Her eyes met his in a dead-on challenge. "Not that you'll ever find out again. But if you're ever curious about how good I am in bed, just ask O'lyn. I'm sure he'd be more than happy to tell you."

Clark froze. She had his full attention now. "What do you mean?"

Veronica smirked. "Well, I have to tell you, you might be great at finding someone's weakness, but O'lyn kicks ass at finding someone's g-spot. You know what a g-spot is right, Clark?" Veronica waved a hand. "What am I saying; of course you don't. We've been married twelve months and you haven't found it, yet!"

Clark stood and slammed his hands down on the table, but Veronica barely moved. She was used to his mood swings. "He touched you?"

Veronica wasn't afraid. She'd been waiting to die all morning and Clark's hesitance to kill her was starting to drag on her nerves. "More than once. Judging by my orgasms, he touched me multiple times."

Clark clenched his fists and gave a humorless smile. "Well then I'm glad I had him killed."

Veronica froze. "What do you mean?"

"Dead," Clark's eyes were ice as he marched around the table. "Your little boyfriend is dead. I gave De 'Carlo the order this morning."

Veronica felt her heart stop. She'd thought she was dead inside before, but that was only an illusion compared to the pain she felt when Clark told her O'lyn was dead. "You promised..."

"And you promised to love, honor and obey me." Clark spat out. "Just what part of that loving and honoring involved fucking our pool boy?"

Veronica couldn't answer him because she couldn't find words. The boy she'd loved forever was dead and her monster of a husband was the man who killed him. If O'lyn hadn't felt the need to apologize, if he never knew her, he would still be alive. It was all her fault. She wanted to die. Dead eyes met her husband's as he came to stand in front of her. "Are you going to kill me yet? Because I have to tell you, every second I'm forced to spend with you is a tortured existence that you will regret."

Clark leaned down over her chair and stared her dead in the eye. "Why would I kill you, Veronica?" Clark leaned in close to her face, twisting her hair around his hand and yanking her head back. "Like you said if you're so damn good at baby making, let's go try for one now."

Veronica screamed as Clark ripped her out of the chair by her hair, yanking her towards the stairs to their bedroom.

"What are you going to do?" O'lyn looked around the car nervously. Aside from the tiger in the trunk, their car was filled with rare and extremely expensive puppies. Killer sat between them, as the crazed criminal mastermind seemed to have a weird attachment to her pet Rotti. There were black Azawakh's in the back seat and a mid-sized poodle lying in the passenger seat.

"You probably don't want to know."

"Who's following us?"

Mech peered into the rearview. "I would know that large sloping forehead anywhere." She smirked at O'lyn. "That tail ain't for me. It's for you. It's De 'Carlo and some of Torres's thugs. My guess would be that they came to finish you off for what you did to their mailbox."

O'lyn nearly exploded. "I didn't smash their mailbox!"

Mech giggled and O'lyn was a little thrown off by such a girlish sound coming from such a non-girlish person. "I know. It was totally me." She laughed again. "I went to drop off a wedding present and my hand slipped." She met his incredulous gaze, looking slightly shamefaced. "I am a terrible driver."

O'lyn shook his head, feeling more than a little annoyed. "Why am I not surprised?"

"Hey, I'm not the one who fucked his wife."

"Touché." O'lyn tossed a nervous look over his shoulder. "So we're really going to take on a bunch of angry thugs; just the two of us?"

Mech nodded. "No way am I telling my uncle I kidnapped the dogs. He was mad enough over Killer." Mech shrugged. "But we'll sort of have help."

"Sort of?" O'lyn was getting even more nervous.

"Do you want your girlfriend back or not?" O'lyn nodded. "Then yes, sort of." Mech peeked out the window as they pulled up next to a crushed yellow Monte Carlo. "We're here."

"Wait, isn't that the..."

"Yes, it's the Columbians' car." She pointed at the warehouse. "Small-time group. Not affiliated and not locals."

"And what does that have to do with our current situation?"

"I'm using your situation to fix my situation." Suddenly, Mech rammed her hand down on the horn of her Capris. After a few seconds, several dark-skinned men popped out of the warehouse. Mech rolled down the window. "Hey fuckers, check out my new collection!" She slammed on the horn again. Killer began howling and the puppies yelped loudly.

"What the fuck are you doing?"

"Trying to get them to chase us," Mech announced as she laid on the horn again.

It only took a second for the Columbians to realize what was going on and they began scrambling to get into their own car, a giant brown Escalade. Mech slammed on the gas.

"Remember the gun?"

O'lyn sighed and popped open the glove compartment. "You're fucking nuts; you know that right?"

"Yup," She nodded at the car in the rearview. "Do not disable their vehicle," Mech informed him definitely as an Escalade pulled up behind them. "Just keep them interested."

O'lyn leaned out the window and began his second round of gunfire in his second Low Country high-speed chase.

"Get the fuck off of me, you bastard," Veronica shrieked as Clark shoved her down on the bed. She squirmed helplessly as Clark restrained her wrists down to the mattress. His face loomed over hers.

"I thought you were good at baby making, Veronica," His voice was mocking and his eyes were amused. "You're so experienced at it, after all."

Clark lowered his head to kiss her and Veronica pulled back. She flexed her neck and, just as his mouth started to cover hers, head-butted him with all her might.

"Fuck!" Clark jumped up and stumbled backwards away from her. He touched his lip, where blood was starting to well. "When the fuck did you get so vicious?"

"Probably the day I saw my husband murder someone with the same carving knife that I used to cut our Thanksgiving turkey." Veronica stared him down from the place she was crouched in her marital bed, waiting for his next attack.

"I told you I was sorry about that." Clark sprung and lunged at her and Veronica rolled away just in time to avoid getting caught.

Veronica backed away as Clark started to stalk her around the bed. "Well that just makes up for everything, then."

Clark watched her like prey, breathing hard. "You don't need to concern yourself about business matters. I've told you that already."

"I do when 'business matters' involve you murdering someone's family." Veronica felt tears prick her eyes as she remembered Herman's destroyed expression after finding out his children had been murdered. She backed away from Clark as he advanced on her. "How could you do that? How could you kill innocent people? How could you murder O'lyn when all he did was give me a ride?"

"He ran over our mailbox," Clark hissed as he took another step towards her.

Veronica took a deep breath. Clark had her pinned into a corner. "So he deserved to die for that? Did Herman deserve to die like that? Does anyone deserve to die like that? Jesus, Clark, you murdered his family. You killed innocent people for nothing more than business and you expect me to be able to have a family for a man like that?" Veronica shook her head as tears filled her eyes. "I'd rather die. I'd rather die than bring a child into the world that is just like you."

Clark clenched his fists as he glared at his wife, cowering in the corner. Her words had cut to the bone and he had nothing left. "Then I guess you have to."

Veronica met his gaze unfeelingly. "It's about fucking time."

Then, all hell broke loose.

O'lyn felt a quiver of excitement when he realized that Mech wasn't planning on stopping at the gate. For at least 20 minutes, he'd been exchanging gunfire with an Escalade without intentionally disabling it. Then he'd learned why.

They were going to the belly of the beast.

Mech burst through the front gates of Veronica's gated community, with both a Lincoln Town car and a brown Escalade hot on their heels. The animals in the car were shrieking and whimpering was starting to give O'lyn a headache.

O'lyn tensed as they started to pull up in front of Veronica's house. Instead of stopping, though, Mech did something he didn't expect. She drove through the front doors he'd been standing in less than 48 hours before.

The perfect French doors burst open as the Capris plowed through them. They weren't even stopped when Mech shoved open her door and rolled onto the floor. O'lyn followed her lead, taking the gun with him. He ducked his head at the Columbians followed them in, their own gunfire and the debris from the crash making the air thick and smoky.

He looked around. Everything was slightly grey with the disturbance of dust and gun smoke in the air. Mech crab walked her way to the driver's side of the door, using the car as cover. O'lyn fired blindly, not caring if he was hitting anything, just wanting to keep up the chaos.

Clark hadn't been expecting a full frontal attack, or any attack at all, for that matter. None of his underlings had been in residence at the time and he was pretty sure De 'Carlo had opted to park his car, rather than drive it into the house. O'lyn and Mech were crouched beside her car. Men swearing in Spanish fired gunshots at them and they were seriously outnumbered. The Columbians were quickly winning the fight and O'lyn wasn't sure what he was supposed to do.

"Ok," Mech smiled, even though she was breathing hard. "I imagine Pearl is good and pissed now." Keeping low, she moved to her Capris and yanked a lever next to the driver's seat of the car, popping open the truck. O'lyn waited for a second, thinking that the tiger had been killed in the crash. Just as he was starting to get worried, the lid flew up and about 240 pounds of seriously furious tiger shot out of the trunk.

The Spanish swears quickly turned to prayers. The tiger focused on one of the smaller men in the group and lunged. They heard a collective scream as all the Columbians scattered at once, some disappearing into the house while one jumped in the Escalade and reversed out of the house and down the street, his screeching tires audible even above the commotion inside. Mech turned a mischievous smile to O'lyn.

"I think it's time to go get your girl. I'll handle things down here."

O'lyn didn't need to be told twice.

Veronica backed up against the far wall, flinching as her husband repeatedly kicked the bathroom door, trying to break it down. She'd taken the commotion downstairs as an opportunity to run, but the farthest she got was her and Clark's bathroom, where she slammed the heavy oak door and locked it behind her.

She didn't know what was going on. Through the door and Clark's furious kicks, she could hear the muffled sound of something that sounded like gun fire and endless crashing. She absently wondered what was going on. The world outside her luxury bathroom sounded like Armageddon. Clark kicked the door again and she flinched. As stoic as she was earlier, she wasn't looking forward to the pain he would inflict on her. Especially now that she knew what he had done to O'lyn. Her sacrifice had been in vain. Her eyes filled with tears and she forced herself to blink them away. Instead, as Clark gave the door another kick that came dangerously close to breaking it down, Veronica began to scour the room for a weapon. She spied one thing she might be able to use in the soap dish of the shower. A tiny, purple razor. She was just wrapping her hand around the plastic handle when the wood of the door hinge finally gave in and burst open.

Veronica spun and watched Clark with wide eyes as he advanced on her. She clutched her razor in a shaking hand and cowered away as he moved towards her.

His eyes were full of fury. "Not so fearless now, are you, you little bitch?" Suddenly, he was on top of her, his hand squeezing her throat. Veronica gasped for air and, in desperation, lashed out with the razor. Clark let out a howl of pain and released her, causing Veronica to slide to the floor. His hand was clutched over his eye and he was bleeding.

Veronica didn't waste time; she raced past her husband, through the broken shards of the door and let out a scream as she crashed into a broad masculine chest.

"Veronica?" O'lyn clutched her upper arms and pulled her back a bit so he could look at her. "Are you okay?"

Veronica could barely speak. She stared up at O'lyn in wonder. "You're alive."

"Just barely, but a bit heartbroken." O'lyn's dark eyes focused on hers. "Why did you take off on me?"

"O'lyn, I..."

"Well isn't this sweet." They both spun to where Clark was coming out of the bathroom, kicking the rubble of the door out of his way, a large gash under his right eye streaming blood. "Your little boyfriend showed up to die with you." Clark took a menacing step towards them and O'lyn shoved Veronica behind him.

"Stay the hell away from her."

Clark smirked. "I don't need to worry about her. De 'Carlo can take care of her when he gets here." Clark cracked his knuckles and took a step forward. "You, I can handle myself. It's the least I owe you for stealing my wife," Clark took another step, "And running over my mailbox."

O'lyn's eyes flashed in rage. He pushed Veronica back out of the line of fire and met Clark's angry gaze dead-on. "I might have stolen your wife, but damn it I didn't run over your mailbox." He lunged at Clark, throwing a punch that caught him square in the jaw and made his head snap back. Clark swore and threw one back and, soon, they were grappling and O'lyn realized he was pretty evenly matched.

O'lyn had been trained by six months of prize fighting in the ring and his hits were clean and focused. Clark had been trained on the streets of the Spanish Harlem and his fighting style was street-taught and vicious. O'lyn jumped back just in time to avoid a knee to the balls and caught another punch in the face for his efforts. He feinted right, which Clark easily blocked, and while he was distracted, nailed him in the stomach.

Clark grunted, doubling over, shoving his way back. He stumbled his way to the nightstand near the bed and O'lyn took a look at Veronica, hovering behind him nervously.

"Enough of this," Clark grunted. He ripped open the drawer, and pulled out a gun.

"Veronica, get the hell out of here." O'lyn cursed himself for leaving his own gun downstairs with Mech. Of course, she was fighting a large group of angry Columbians...and a Siberian Tiger, but still.

"I'm not leaving you, O'lyn."

O'lyn sighed over her stubbornness, starting to walk backwards out of the room. She struggled to get around him, but he wouldn't let her.

Clark gave a cruel smile as he backed them into the hallway. "It's okay; I have enough bullets for both of you."

Veronica's back hit the railing of the stairs and they were forced to stop. She wrapped her arms around O'lyn's waist, waiting for the bullet. Then she heard a growl.

"Is that a tiger?" Veronica noticed at the same time Clark and O'lyn did. It was surreal. A large white tiger sat in her upstairs hallway. "Nobody move." She whispered breathlessly. "If you run, it will think you're prey. Just hold still."

O'lyn listened. He slipped his hand over hers and squeezed tightly.

Clark didn't. Instead, he turned the gun on the tiger and fired a shot. He missed by a mile and only succeeded in pissing it off. Then, Clark panicked and did the worst possible thing in the world he could have.

He turned his back and ran. The confused beast was immediately in predator mode, focusing its angry eyes on Clark's back. In a split second decision O'lyn pushed Clark out of the way as the tiger leapt in the air.

Veronica let out a horrified scream as she watched her husband fall backward letting off two rounds into the airborne tiger. The blood spurted and, despite the hatred she felt for her husband, deep inside she felt the pain of him almost dying at the hands of the beast. He struggled to push the dead animal off him while still holding onto the weapon. Veronica began to pull O'lyn with her, tugging him towards the stairs. They both backed down quietly and, for the first time, Veronica noticed the bedlam that was going on in the place she'd once called home.

"What the hell?" She gasped as she looked around the room. Killer the Rottweiler held a large Columbian man hostage behind a chair, as Mech crouched down behind the door of her Capris.

O'lyn smiled wryly. "As you can probably tell, I went to Mech for help when I found out you were gone."

"You went to Mech?" Veronica turned to O'lyn with shock on her face. "You? I thought you thought she was insane"

"She is insane," O'lyn emphasized as he wrapped his arms around Veronica, "But I would have gone to Satan if it meant helping you."

Veronica tried to pull back. "I think you might be taking this guilt thing a bit too far."

"Veronica ..." O'lyn didn't get time to finish his sentence because Mech came screaming from behind the car, De 'Carlo hot on her heels.

"Rot in hell, you Mexican bastard. You Latin reject!" Mech let out a laugh and fired in De 'Carlo's general direction, jumping and sliding over the hood of her Capris. De 'Carlo stopped mid-chase, frozen in shock to see O'lyn still alive.

"Pool boy!" he hissed, starting to march his way up the stairs.

O'lyn shook his head in confusion as he prepared to do battle with De 'Carlo again. "Why does everyone keep calling me that?"

Veronica gave O'lyn a once over. "You do look a little like our pool boy."

"Really?"

Veronica nodded, "Older though. And cuter."

"Enough!" De 'Carlo's shout brought them back to their predicament. O'lyn started to shove Veronica behind him again, preparing for another fight. Then, De 'Carlo's ascent was halted by the arrival of a new party. The hiding Columbian man had seen him, knowing the threat of the tiger was gone, and come out from behind the piano.

"Punta!" the man hissed as he came out from behind the piano, "It was you who is stealing the animals from our operations."

From somewhere beside the Capris, Veronica would've sworn she heard Mech giggle.

De 'Carlo spun, seeming to notice the Columbians in the house for the first time. "What are you talking about?"

Mech popped up from where she was hiding behind the car. "Hey De 'Carlo." She had put down her gun and picked up something much bigger. "Here's that Azawakh you told me to steal." She held the puppy up over her head. Then, suddenly, almost in slow motion, she tossed it in his direction.

De 'Carlo let out a girlish squeal and ducked, but he was too slow. The dog landed on his face and the Columbian wasn't far behind.

"Well," Mech brushed herself off and walked around the car, "That takes care of him." She started to walk towards Veronica and O'lyn when the last standing Columbian raised his gun.

"You pay for this, Punta." Mech turned and her eyes widened. She'd left her gun on the floor and kept her face focused on the Columbians. Mech's eyes trained on the Columbian and an eerier smile crossed her face. Mech raised her arms in defeat before crossing her eyes, she angled her head to the left knowing the Columbian's eyes would follow in the same direction. Before the Columbian could assess what was taking place Veronica filled his chest with three shots from Mech's gun.

CHAPTER

EIGHT

A COUPLE HOURS LATER, Veronica was finished with statements and interviews. The remaining Columbians were taken into custody. In a panic, Veronica placed assault charges against Clark and he was arrested. The crime scene detective assured her she would be able to get a restraining order against him and suggested she find another residence.

During the three hours of questions, Veronica played stupid. She claimed no knowledge of any criminal enterprise and the detectives had apparently bought it.

Neither O'lyn nor Mech's name had come up. Instead, the police determined that her husband had been attacked by a small organized crime syndicate, after they'd determined that Clark refused to turn over the warehouse space on the docks. Animal control was called in to take care of all the puppies and Veronica informed them Killer was her pet.

The police told Veronica she might be called on to testify in court, but wasn't sure. Most of the involved parties were dead. There was probably nothing to testify about.

Veronica played the role of shell-shocked, slightly ditzy wife well and she was allowed to call a friend to pick her up. She called O'lyn, who snuck away with Mech only hours before.

"You okay."

Veronica nodded numbly. She was free and she was alive. The events of the day were almost blurry. They felt like they happened to someone else. "I should feel something," She looked in confusion at O'lyn. "I was married to the man for twelve months. I should feel something."

O'lyn rested his hand on her knee. "You're probably still in shock."

Veronica shook her head. "It's more than that. It's like I never felt anything for him." She blinked back tears. "I liked him well enough. I knew he could take care of me, but in twelve months of marriage, I never felt for him what it took me one night to feel..." Veronica   stopped, afraid of saying too much. O'lyn was free now, too. He'd more than made up for one horrible insult in high school. "Look, O'lyn…"

O'lyn put up a hand. "What were you going to say?"

Veronica shook her head again. "It doesn't matter."

Veronica's body shot forward in her seat as O'lyn slammed on the brakes. "It matters."

Veronica let out a frustrated groan. "It doesn't, O'lyn. It was one night. Sure, I felt something, but I've had a crush on you since high school. I was bound to feel something." Tears blurred her vision. "I know you feel guilty, like what's happening in my life is your fault, but it's not. You don't need to take care of me, anymore. I have friends; they can help me."

"That's not why I'm doing this, Veronica."

Veronica spun towards him in her seat. "Then why? Why are you doing this, O'lyn, because I have to tell you, I can't take it any longer? Your guilt is making me feel guilty and the guiltier I feel, the guiltier you act until it just gets worse and worse and I don't know how to make you understand that it's okay now. I'm going to be okay."

"I'm doing this because of what I said that night. You belong with me, Veronica. You always have." O'lyn clenched the steering wheel, unable to look at Veronica. "I was an idiot in high school. When you were tutoring me, I was getting more and more attached to you every day. But you stayed so detached, it was driving me crazy. Of all the girls in school, I had a crush on the one who would turn me down for a date for a book lecture."

Veronica shook her head. "That's ridiculous. You didn't like me like that."

O'lyn snorted. "Really?" He glared at her. "I'd been struggling with how to ask you out for a week. Then, when you came in for tutoring, I built up my courage and I asked you to come to my game." He shot her a look, "Do you remember that?"

"Yeah," Veronica nodded at the hazy memory. "You told me you were playing that night. I thought you were just making conversation."

"I wanted you to watch me play," O'lyn nearly shouted. "Instead, you told me you already had plans; that you were going to the damn lecture. I just wanted you to see me doing something I was actually good at instead of thinking I was just some dumb jock. Instead, you told me that you were spending the evening at a book festival and because some author was going to give a lecture."

"It was Omar Tyree!" Veronica shook her head. "There was limited seating for the event and I had saved to get a ticket for months. Plus, football is boring."

"Well, you're going to have to learn to love it." O'lyn didn't give Veronica time to ask what he meant by that. "After that, I was so damn mad at you, and my friends kept making fun of me. I thought it would be perfect revenge – to prove that you wanted me. I played that stupid prank," O'lyn blinked back tears and his voice caught a little, "and then I never saw you again."

"The school let me do the rest of my classes from home after that." Veronica whispered. "The semester was almost over, anyway, and my mom was really sick."

"You never told me that. You never told me anything about you."

Veronica's breath hitched. "It was too hard to talk about. Whenever I mentioned it, it just felt too real. We–" Veronica blinked, "My whole family knew she was terminal. But she wanted to pretend everything was normal. O'lyn, it was a hard time for me. I barely knew what I was thinking, myself. And you were the king of the high school. I didn't think you wanted me. I didn't think anyone would want me." Veronica sucked in a deep breath. "The truth is, I was crazy about you, but I was too afraid to admit it. For me, things were easier when they were bad. Hope and daydreams just ended in disappointment." She swallowed again. "They still do." Veronica pushed a hand through her hair. "I picked Clark because he was easy. He would take care of me and he was too distant to get attached to. He felt safe. I felt safe. I just couldn't bear the thought of losing someone I loved again."

O'lyn reached over, starling Veronica as he clutched her hand. "I'm sorry. I was a selfish asshole. I never thought of what you were going through. I was just pissed that I could get any girl in the school I wanted, but

I couldn't have you." He pressed Veronica's hand to his mouth. "For years, the look on your face stayed with me. No matter what I saw, it was your sad grey-green eyes that stayed with me. I thought that I just felt guilty. I told myself that you'd gotten ugly and fat when you got older. I told myself you were living in a trailer with eight kids. I told myself anything I could to convince myself that you didn't belong with me; that I hadn't ruined the one chance I'd had at love, because it's true. You're the only woman I ever loved." He ignored Veronica's gasp and kept talking. "I was just going to find you; to see for myself that you were a happy, boring housewife. Instead," he gestured at Veronica, "you were a goddess with a Spanish drug-dealing husband." O'lyn pressed her hand to his mouth again. "I made a mistake back then, Veronica, but I'm not making it now. I meant what I said that night. You belong with me. You're supposed to be mine."

"O'lyn," Veronica choked out the words. "I don't..."

O'lyn turned towards her and tugged her into his arms. "I know it's scary and I know that you've been through a lot, but I'm not risking losing you again. I loved you then and I love you now, Veronica. If you need some time to get used to that, I understand. I'll keep my hands to myself. But I'm not letting you go." O'lyn shook his head. "Not now that I've found you again. Because I'm right; we belong together."

Veronica swallowed nervously. "Not even for a second during my marriage did I feel the way about Clark how I did about you for one night. That's what I was going to say." Veronica took a deep breath. "I didn't go back to him because I loved him. The truth is I never loved him. But I've always loved you." She pressed herself against him, enjoying the heat from his body. "I've always loved you."

O'lyn lowered his head to her. "Well, it's about damn time that you admitted that." He pressed his lips down onto hers and forgot about the past.

CHAPTER

NINE

CLARK LISTENED calmly while the officer informed him he would be taking a detour through the warehouse district before going to the station. He needed him to understand the remaining events of the day could go one of two ways. His sharp features hardened while he talked. He knew the officers on his payroll and this wasn't one of them. He twisted his bound wrist slightly trying to relieve the pressure leading down to his fingers. The officer began speaking again, informing Clark that Lieutenant Michaels was waiting on the docks for him.

A short while later, the officer pulled into the dock warehouse. Lieutenant Michaels was there waiting with a badly injured De 'Carlo. Furious, he rose; he was a big man, moving like a jungle cat just spotting his prey. "I told you to kill that bastard! But instead he ends up inside my living room. I should kill you right now." Clark sneered.

"He wasn't there Clark. We tossed the motel room and then headed to the Brake Pad. We spotted Mech's car and followed them. She went to the Columbians area and started a chase with them. That's how we ended up in the living room."

Clark paced furiously while the Lieutenant watch De 'Carlo nervously. "You both know that whatever you did to bring this on, someone has to take the fall. We can't just arrest the Columbians without one of you going down along with them." Clark stopped dead in his tracks and looked from De 'Carlo to the lieutenant. "Take him and Marcus. They are of no use to me right now. I want you to find my wife and the fucking pool boy." Clark paused in thought. "She's a lot feistier than I ever knew. After I take care of that fucking pool boy, she'll be taught how I handle my business." Clark stated.

De 'Carlo took a step backwards grateful his life wouldn't end today. He hunched away from Clark, his shoulders stiffening as he exhaled the breaths he had been holding from the moment Clark stepped out of the car. Lieutenant Michaels pressed the remote control, activating the door to the adjacent building. He tossed the keys to Clark and told him the cargo barge leaving in the hour would take him to Colonel's Island, where a pontoon was awaiting his arrival. Little Sea Island housed his private residence. The house had been recently restocked and he knew he could remain there until things cooled back down.

Clark smiled for the first time thinking it would be good to recoup with his island mistress. He turned to the Lieutenant, before he could ask he nodded. "Yes, she's been informed of your forthcoming arrival.

Clark made his way from the darkened warehouse into the separate room. Surveying the space, he seized three hefty leather duffle bags. Unzipping each bag, he checked the contents thoroughly ensuring each were labeled properly. He tossed the first bag to the Lieutenant knowing that it was more than enough to cover the expenses he'd racked up in the day's events. The remaining two bags, he threw over his shoulders and made his way to the cargo barge.

EPILOGUE

O'lyn and Veronica walked hand in hand into the Brake Pad, their clothes still slightly rumpled from their roadside tryst. Mech's middle-aged uncle Beast was behind the bar, fixing himself a mid-afternoon drink.

All eyes were on Mech as she entered the room, studying the faces around her bar. Her usually untamed hair was now bone straight and auburn. She looked completely different.

"Well don't just stand there with your mouths open...pour me up a drink too Beast." She stated while flipping her hair.

"Wow, Mech. You look great!" O'lyn nodded along.

Veronica sucked in a breath. "We just stopped by before leaving town. O'lyn and I are going to head up to Memphis or maybe head to Seattle."

"I'm leaving as well, there a spot on South Beach that has my name on it." Mech stated. I'm glad you stopped by, here's some parting gifts and something to hold you over until you get settled. Veronica, you might wanna handle your divorce as soon as you're settled.

The flat assertion sent a small shiver skimming down her spine, and if she had any further doubts, they were abruptly erased. O'lyn placed his hands around her waist pulling her closer to him. He could still feel her shivering slightly. She feared she'd lose control right then in there.

From the moment she slid in the attic closet her life had changed drastically. But now standing here with O'lyn she felt more empowered, more female and stronger than ever.

She rubbed her palm up over the side of O'lyn's jaw and surrendered the ties that held her to Clark with one exhaling breathe.

"Are you sure you want to do this?"

Veronica nodded, "I've never been surer."

They finished their goodbyes with Mech and walked out of the Brake Pad. O'lyn gunned the engine and pulled out into the street.

"I hope you're not still feeling guilty..."

O'lyn smiled. "Do I need to pull over and show you how not guilty I feel? Veronica blushed and smiled. "No, but you could kiss me again."

O'lyn chuckled and put on the brakes, pulling over to the side of the road. He tugged Veronica into his arms and lowered his mouth to meet hers. His lips brushed against hers gently and Veronica clutched his shirt, pulling him closer. He kissed her until she was dizzy, finally pulling back, gasping and watching her with dilated pupils. "How was that?"

ACKNOWLEDGMENTS

I started this book with a memory I had from Jr. High School. Bullying is the use of force, threat, or coercion to abuse, intimidate, verbal or aggressively impose domination over others. The behavior is often repeated and habitual. You don't have to suffer alone. If you feel you have been bullied, get help. Tell someone. Never suffer the ridicule alone. For additional resources go to www.stopbullying.gov

Dear TRZ friends:

I'm sending you this little note to let you know how much I appreciate and value your friendship. Anytime I am going through a rough patch, you were there to lift me up with your wise words, and comfort me with your hugs. Thank you so much for being there for me. And I want you to know that if there ever comes a time you need someone to lean on, you can definitely count on me! ~*Red*

To my readers, I would like to mention each and every one of you, but I am afraid I would forget someone's name.   So INSERT YOUR NAME HERE:

I love you so much. Thank you. I am inspired daily from the smallest of things. Thank you for taking time to read my works and recommending me to your friends.

Always, LaRedeaux

ABOUT THE AUTHOR

I Write stories to entertain and offer a temporary escape into another life. I create interesting characters who may linger with the reader long after they have finished the story. Some stories examine lives, motivations, hopes and fears and the courage to change. I write about the everyday stuff, but with a fictional twist.

I Write about the four L's: *life, love, lust and lies* – including the lies we tell ourselves. And yes, I want to change the world. A little tiny bit of it, anyway.

Add more books by *LaRedeaux* to your reading list.

www.midnightpublications.com

www.laredeaux.com

www.amazon.com/author/laredeaux